GRASS MEANS FIGHT

Center Point
Large Print

GRASS MEANS FIGHT

KIRK DEMING

CENTER POINT LARGE PRINT
THORNDIKE, MAINE

This Center Point Large Print edition
is published in the year 2025 by arrangement with
Golden West Inc.

Copyright © 1938 by The Macaulay Company.

All rights reserved.

The text of this Large Print edition is unabridged.
In other aspects, this book may vary
from the original edition.
Printed in the United States of America
on permanent paper sourced using
environmentally responsible foresting methods.
Set in 16-point Times New Roman type.

ISBN: 979-8-89164-609-4

The Library of Congress has cataloged this record
under Library of Congress Control Number: 2025934464

1

Kirk Jordan and Pecos Johnson came riding together across spreading sage range toward the Wagon Wheel ranch house. The clear, tinted horizon of the New Mexican sky made a vivid backdrop for their silhouetted forms.

They were a strange combination. Always together when the circumstances of their work permitted, they were partners, more than friends, despite their difference in age, in appearance, and in the plain signs of their origin.

Standing in his shirtsleeves on the ranch house gallery, his shrewd eyes slitted as he watched them come, old Clem Chew caught his nether lip between his teeth and shook his head at some thought of his own.

He did not change position as they neared, his glance following them into the yard to the corrals. They took care of their broncs. A moment later they came striding up toward the house.

Kirk Jordan was tall, lean, black-headed and grey-eyed, in his middle twenties; handsome in a vigorous, healthy way. His clear skin was tanned almost to redness by wind-beat and the pound of an ardent sun. Little escaped his keen scrutiny.

Breeding showed unmistakably in his heritage and in the way he handled his body; good blood and the assurance of a fighting heart. He had drifted west as a boy, made it his home. He never referred to the past.

His six feet of rawhide sinew was a strange contrast to Pecos Johnson's gnarled and rugged five-foot-two. The little man—he was all of forty-five—wore a ragged mustache across that leathery, hard-bitten and somehow uncompromising face out of which looked bleak, unwavering eyes. If he hobbled slightly it was because his bowed legs had been broken in a dozen places under falling horses.

The pair joined Clem on the gallery. For some minutes the talk was of range and water, the details of stock handling on this far-flung ranch, as big as some Eastern counties but no novelty for New Mexico. Then Chew hesitated, cleared his throat in an embarrassed way, and finally said:

"I'm sorry to have to tell yuh this, but there ain't no help for it. . . . The place is sold."

Arrested, they stared unbelievingly, their brows contracted in amazement. Johnson, at least, skeptically scented some little joke. Clem Chew was a waggish old coot. He had owned the Wagon Wheel for nearly a score of years, carving it out of wild territory not at all safe from marauding Apaches from over west. The pockmarks of Indian bullets still showed in the adobe walls of his home.

Kirk and Pecos had been with him for the last four or five of those years, putting their own salary back into stock until a good hundred head of J Bar steers, their joint property, now grazed the Wagon Wheel range. In all that time Clem had never breathed a word of any intention to sell.

Pecos was the first to break this freighted silence. "What yuh mean, sold?" he grunted.

Clem spread his rope-scarred hands.

"This ain't no trick, boys," he said hurriedly. "I didn't aim to hold off speakin' up so long, but I wanted to make shore first . . . You've seen Gabe Within here two-three times lately, huh? He's certain of election to the Territorial Congress, he says; an' it's give him ambitions. He's gettin' rid of his little Carrizo spread an' has been wantin' the Wagon Wheel, as bein' more suitable to the importance of his position. I can't say I cottoned to the notion much, but he talked me into it. We signed the papers this mornin'—"

"What about you, Clem?" Kirk Jordan queried quietly. "What'll you do?"

"Wal, I'm goin' East," Chew answered his question in a flustered way. He felt keenly that he had let these two down in some way. "I'm gettin' old. My daughter back in Illinoy wants me to come live with her."

"Daughter?" Pecos barked. He was bristling now. "I never heard you had no daughter."

"Wal, I have!" old Clem was quick to retort.

"When's Within taking over?" Kirk asked Clem.

"End of the month."

"Buying stock, brand and all, eh?"

"Yeh—"

"That means we got less'n ten days to cut out our J Bar stuff an' drift it along," Pecos grumbled.

"—Unless yuh want to sell out to Within along with me," Clem put in. "I reckon he'd buy yore bunch if yuh was to say the word."

The eyes of Kirk and Pecos met. Each was mutely asking the other's opinion of that move. Then Kirk said slowly: "We'll think it over and make up our minds sometime during the day."

No more was said of the matter then, but later, when they were alone, Pecos spoke his mind.

"I reckon Clem's got a right to do what he wants. But it means move on fer us," he averred. "Question is: do we scratch fer another job—or do what we've always said we'd do someday?"

Kirk's answer was unhesitating: "I'm for locating a range of our own. Then the next time we move on it'll be because we want to."

Pecos eyed him soberly, lines of thought in his worn, leathery cheeks. He had Kirk Jordan's best interests at heart, as he had had from the day the latter, little more than a lanky youngster then, had pulled him out of the boiling, bank-full Red River.

The little man hoped never to see Kirk become

the directionless drifter he had been. Something leaped in him at this unmistakable sign that the urge was working in the other to settle down. Someday Kirk would marry, raise a family and be somebody. Pecos meant to help him all he could. He nodded unemotionally.

"We'll do that, then."

On communicating their intentions to old Clem, the rancher promptly released them from other duties. They threw themselves into the task of gathering their J Bar beef. A week to the day from the time they started, a hundred and eighteen head were bunched, ready to drive.

"Ain't no point in hangin' around here the day or two till Gabe Within takes over," old Clem told them that night. "I'll make out yore time an' yuh can drag it in the mornin'. . . . Kinda wish I was headin' out with yuh," he added ruefully. Their regret at leaving the Wagon Wheel was nothing to his feelings on quitting the cattle business altogether.

Accordingly, in the grey of the following morning they were astir. Breakfast was a silent affair. There were no pointed farewells, only a trio of tight-lipped "So longs." These men understood one another. Kirk and Pecos got their little herd headed out. Before the sun peeped over the shadow-gashed range to the east, the Wagon Wheel buildings had dropped out of sight to the rear.

By common consent they were driving into the west. It was wild land over there, much of it unclaimed. Beyond leagues of broken desert country the endless barrier mountains of Arizona loomed against the sky.

To the southeast, range wars made conditions uncertain. North hovered the shadow of advancing settlement. West lay their only course.

The first day was the most arduous for man and beast. After that they dropped into the routine of the trail. Miles of an incredible roughness rolled behind.

On the third day they struck desert with a vengeance. Fortunately they were able to water the stock on its edge. They forced on then without delay. Night found them amidst a desolate waste, with no hint of an end, no slightest sign of water.

"What yuh think?" Pecos queried. "Shall we bed down?"

"Keep 'em moving!" Kirk called out. "No telling how we'll come out of this. The going will be easier on the steers than in that blazing sun, at any rate."

They shoved ahead, weary and dogged. In the small hours, though no water had been scented, they hauled up at last. The stock was gaunted. Kirk knew that rest was the best thing for them, in the few cool hours remaining before the dawn.

Daylight found them on the trail again. It was

mid-morning before any break came in the deadly sameness surrounding them. They had traversed nearly a hundred miles of desert. Arizona seemed close now. Its darkly timbered swells bulked up beyond bastion walls of dull red rock.

They followed the wall till a break let them through.

"We're near out of it now," Pecos predicted, with relief. "Ought to strike grass in 'nother couple hours."

He spoke too soon. Over a mesquite-cluttered rise a desert basin opened up before them, sere and brown. But its shoulders lifted to high, cool range. And through its middle straggled a line of what had once been fine cottonwoods.

"Hello! Some kind of an outfit down there," Pecos exclaimed. "How-come anybody'd build here? There ain't no grass in miles of the place."

"I see it." Kirk was gazing that way, his mind busy with the puzzle. "We'll head down. Ought to get water there anyway."

Indeed, the steers had already winded it. They tossed their horns and quickened their pace. The two punchers let them go, making sure only that they kept to open ground.

The ranch drew near. It was a cracked and weathered old place, crying for moisture. Nobody appeared at once. The J Bar steers headed for a clump of trees amidst which a tank appeared. Water was there, waiting. But before the stock reached it, it came full tilt against a stout fence closing it out.

"I'll hunt for the gate," Pecos said.

"Hold on!" Kirk was curt. "We'll stop at the house first. That's no more than fair. It's my guess that water comes high in this country."

They rode toward the decaying house. As they drew up a lanky, white-haired old fellow stepped out. His slitted eyes ran over them calculatingly.

"Howdy."

It was a noncommittal greeting. Kirk dropped a nod.

"Driftin' some stock through?"

"Yeh. A hundred head. We're lookin' for water."

"I sell it," said the old man briefly.

Kirk and Pecos understood the presence of the fence now. Their glances crossed. They had their last pay checks from Clem Chew; but it would take money to start an outfit of their own. They could afford to spend none for water. Kirk thought swiftly.

"All right. Let us water our stock. We're looking for range. We won't be far from here. Soon's we're able we'll come back and square with you."

"Nothin' doin'!" The old-timer was resolute. "No money, no water. That's flat."

Pecos reddened. "Why, dang yore ornery hide—!" he burst out.

"Never mind!" The other's voice rose. "I'm

12

doin' this because I have to. Nobody can say Eph Gowan ever pulled a dirty deal—an' nobody ever put nothin' over on him, neither!"

Kirk was quick to read the situation. This apparently had once been a prosperous ranch. Then drought had struck at it. Now, in all probability, water was the only thing in the world Gowan had to sell. Kirk had seen no cattle whatever.

Yet they were in desperate case. The next water might be miles away. The J Bar steers had to have water if they were to go on.

Pecos saw it too. Wrath boiling up in him, he did not propose to be balked. Before another word was uttered, his Colt flashed out. It trained on Gowan's middle.

"Sorry to disagree with yuh, Pop; but we're gettin' water, an' we're gettin' it now!" he bit off, grimly.

Gowan did not move. Nor did his face change. "No yuh ain't!" he flung back. "I been here fer fifteen years, an' I'm still here! Who in hell are yuh, to come driftin' along an' tell me what to do?"

Pecos's face hardened. His knuckle whitened on the hammer of his six-gun.

"There ain't no use of foolin' with that shootin' iron!" Gowan drove on severely. "You'll never git the hammer back. I got a man inside who's had yuh both covered all the time—pull trigger an' it'll be you the lead tears through!"

Danger sang along Kirk's nerves. But it did not alter their situation.

"Keep him covered, Pecos!" he snapped. "I don't reckon he's lying, but we'll find out. Either we make a play here, or kiss the steers good-bye!"

At the words, a tinkle of breaking glass was heard. Kirk froze. A rifle barrel jutted from a window. It covered Pecos.

Pecos prudently refrained from action. The bitter-voiced old desert rancher met his gaze unflinchingly, challengingly. But when his boring eyes shifted to Kirk Jordan they softened with a new light. So this man was on the drift, eh? For months past all counting, Eph Gowan had been on the lookout for just such a man. Having the urgent use for him that he had, he did not propose to let the opportunity get away now. Suddenly he relaxed.

"Shucks," he grunted gruffly. "Go open the gate an' water yore cows. We'll talk this over!"

2

When Pecos opened the gate in the heavy fence enclosing the water, he was almost knocked down by the rush of steers through the opening.

Inside was a sizeable pool, its edges trampled and muddy. In the rush for the water, the steers pushed some of their number in to their bellies. The moaning bellows gave place to the sound of drinking. There was enough for all.

"Kinda queer deal here," Pecos commented to Kirk in a low tone. "I dunno's I savvy it plumb through."

"Yeh." Kirk was sententious. "Gowan changed front kind of sudden. We'll see if we can find out why."

They headed back for the house. Old Eph was waiting for them on the porch.

"Reckon our broncs can stand a waterin' too," Pecos remarked. He gathered up the reins.

"Never mind that," Gowan told him equably. "You don't have to bother. . . . Straight!" he called.

A dusky figure came shuffling out of the house. He was dressed in crumpled dungarees, a dirty khaki shirt and shapeless felt hat. His long black hair, thick as a broomtail's mane, fell to his shoulders. Kirk gave this man a cursory glance, then looked again, sharply. The other was plainly an Apache.

"Straight Tongue, water them hosses fer the boys," Gowan directed easily. "They're kinda tuckered."

The Indian's visage might have been carved from mahogany heartwood, so unchanging was the bitter, iron expression there. He made no reply. Nor did he glance at Kirk or Pecos. His carbine still in his grasp, he led the ponies toward the tank.

"So yore lookin' fer range, huh?" Gowan began, in quizzical fashion. "Figgerin' to ranch it a while, I reckon."

Kirk assented. "Didn't know there was so much desert over this way."

"Wal, yuh don't have to go much farther. This is about the tail end of it, travelin' west. I got good cause to know."

Kirk was eying Gowan curiously. "I thought this was a cow ranch when I first spotted it."

Gowan nodded, musing. Something hard and grim stole into his features. "It was—a real ranch," he rasped.

"Was?" Pecos echoed, his brows knit. "It don't look it. What happened?"

"The grass died." Gowan communed with himself somberly for a second, then roused. "Yuh'd never guess it, but there was a time when I ran a flourishin' brand in this basin. Quarter-

16

Circle Z. Good, grassy range all over these bottoms in them days." His eye lighted up as he dwelt briefly on the glories of the past, then dulled again to sober reality.

Pecos grunted sympathetically. "Desert jest moved plumb in on yuh, huh?"

"Not only that." Gowan's tone grated again. "Range-grabbin' accounted fer my herd—wiped me out little by little." His sharp glance flamed with remembered hatred and strife. "There was a big owner, grazed over half-a-hundred square miles of this country—forty or fifty punchers ridin' fer him—name of Hutchinson—"

"Cole Hutchinson?" Kirk leaned forward unconsciously. That name had meaning for him. It had been a by-word in the Territory for years as a synonym for power. Clem Chew had talked endlessly about the man. Wary of big outfits, Kirk had never bothered to learn precisely where Hutchinson's huge Ladder outfit was situated. Somewhere over west, was all he had known.

"Yeh, that's him." Gowan's tobacco-stained teeth tugged at his mustache. "Cole Hutchinson an' me had it out, hammer an' tongs, fer several seasons. Men died on both sides. The result was foregone. He had five riders to my one. If I could'a got close 'nough, I'd've blasted him! But slow an' shore, he shoved me back, run my steers off the open range, finished me!" His look was savage.

"Didn't do him no good, though," he resumed, with harsh satisfaction. "Almost before he'd got done smashin' me, the desert come closin' in. In one season alone there was half-a-dozen of the worst sandstorms I ever laid eyes on. It wiped out the grass. Hutchinson drew every hoof an' horn back out of the basin. He gave in—licked by somethin' stronger than him. But I stayed!"

Pecos, at least, was unimpressed. "What did yuh git out of it," he grunted.

Old Eph stabbed him with burning gaze. "Not much in dollars an' cents, mebby. But I was a thorn under Cole Hutchinson's hide! I'd sworn to square with him. . . . Never a head of stock did he drive through this basin from that day on! I'd sell water to most anybody that needed it. Not him! . . . He sent in his gun-throwin' thugs two-three times—come once himself. He wanted to git rid of me if he had to smoke me out, an' then grab my water. But it didn't work!"

"How come he didn't smoke yuh?" Pecos insisted skeptically. "Yuh must've had to let yore crew go, with nothin' but water-sellin' to live on here—"

Gowan did not answer directly. But as Straight Tongue, the Indian, returned to the house, Eph watched him through hawk-lidded eyes. Kirk read the answer in that intent regard. Apaches! They had been Gowan's allies, perhaps in return for some great service in the past. They would have made a formidable foe even in the face of Cole Hutchinson's ruthless might.

Gowan's tension relaxed. "But shucks," he attempted to throw off the shadow of the past, "no point in draggin' out old scores. We started out to talk about you. There's any acreage of fine graze up in them high hills back of the basin. Why don't yuh go up in there an' pick yoreselves a spread?"

"How come?" Pecos demanded. "Accordin' to yore own tell, there's been fightin' all over the place around here fer range. How's it happen nobody's got that good graze up in the hills? An' why ain't you up there?"

Gowan grew wary. "When the desert came in here, it changed the picture considerable," he growled. "As fer me, I'm stayin here fer reasons of my own."

"Well—" said Kirk. "I haven't any objection to taking a look up through the hills. We're drifting that way anyway. But I expect that settling there would mean a fight."

"Good range anywhere means fight, don't it?" Gowan caught him up thinly, his glance probing. "Yuh don't either of yuh look like that'd trouble yuh any."

Pecos looked unconvinced, and Kirk noncommittal. Eph went on to describe the range in the hills in considerable detail. He made it sound

19

undeniably enticing, nor was this without design. If there was any means by which he could direct these men against Cole Hutchinson, he meant to do it.

As he talked on, elaborating the advantages of the upper range, the lines in Pecos's seamed face began to smooth out in approval. He shot a look at Kirk, feeling out his reaction to what they heard.

"Reckon we better ride up there, anyway," he said tentatively.

"I can send along one of my—uh—Straight Tongue can show yuh the way, if you want," Gowan corrected himself.

"Thanks. We'll make out, as long as we strike grass an' water," Kirk responded.

In midafternoon, with the sun already beginning to swing down the western arc of the sky, Kirk and Pecos got the little J Bar bunch headed across the basin toward the first slopes of the tawny hills.

The shadows were darkening by the time they reached the pines. The air here was deliciously cool. There was a fragrant aroma of growing things on the vagrant breeze. The cattle smelled grass in lush quantities.

Through a stand of pine they broke upon a broad, park-like meadow, soothing to the sight even under this copper sky. Beyond another belt of trees, another inviting grazing area. The land here was rolling, rich. The eyes of both men brightened.

"By golly, this is somethin'!" Pecos averred.

"Worth hunting for," Kirk seconded, a hint of reserve in his tone. "I'd about given up expecting to locate anything like it."

Kirk's wariness was not unfounded. As dusk sifted through the trees, without any warning whatever a single rider detached himself from the shadows and sat his saddle, gazing at them out of a blank, expressionless face.

He was a lithe, craggy individual, young but hard-bitten.

Nearing, Kirk could not fail to note the absence of a greeting. He drew in facing the other.

Words dropped from the fellow's thin, almost motionless lips. "Drivin' through?"

Kirk eased in the saddle, rolling this over in his mind.

"Maybe."

The other's brow lifted slightly. "Yuh better," he suggested colorlessly.

Kirk's glance was steady. "Speakin' for somebody?"

"Maybe. Take a tip, cowboy. Keep travelin'."

"So? Maybe you'd like to tell me why."

"Keep hazin' 'em along, an' there'll be no need to go into that. If there ain't no other way. Trouble for us'll be double trouble for you."

Pecos had ridden on. But glancing back, he saw

21

that Kirk was still in converse with the stranger, and turned his horse.

Before he neared, the stranger lifted his reins.

"Any good water handy by here?" Kirk pursued, seeing the puncher about to ride back into the trees.

There was no direct answer. "Be seein' yuh," the man dropped, tight-lipped. There was something of grim promise in the words.

"Who was that?" Pecos queried sharply as he neared.

"Don't know."

"What'd he want?"

"Well—it was some kind of a warnin' he was handing us. Asked me to keep going. I don't know why."

"Uh-huh!" Pecos was terse. "Reckon I expected that. But not so soon . . . Wal—" Pecos hauled his bronc's head around. "We better be thinkin' about a place to bed down. It'll take some ridin' in the mornin' to hit on just the place we're huntin' for."

Kirk's silence gave assent. Together they rode after the J Bar steers. The latter had scented water at last, and were moving straight toward it.

3

They bedded down in an open meadow through which a small stream flowed.

In the morning they pushed on. By mid-morning they came to an enclosed, rolling basin. Pausing at its rim, while the J Bar steers streamed on down, they knew they had come at last to their future ranch.

The basin covered perhaps half-a-dozen square miles. Although composed for the most part of open grazing range of a high order, it was bisected several ways by thinly wooded ridges. Its entire circumference were hemmed in by pine clad heights. To the north the rocky, bulging flanks of Geronimo Mountain jutted into the blue.

"I reckon this is it," said Pecos, with quiet satisfaction. "There's a good-sized crick over there through the trees. Nothin' could be better suited to our purpose."

Kirk agreed. "But we won't figure to bite off the whole basin till we get a line on the stack-up here. We'll shove over," he decided, "and take a look at that far flank, where the creek comes down."

Accordingly they worked across the basin and up under the bulking loom of Geronimo till a natural rocky gateway in a barrier ridge let them through beside the creek into a vast, sloping meadow which was a grazing range in itself.

"This'll do," Pecos declared. "We can slap a pine gate across the rocks, here, an' our fencin's done for the time bein'."

"That's the ticket," Kirk approved. "We'll find a flat along the creek to run up a cabin on, and a couple of corrals."

They wasted no time. The steers drifted out and began to graze, well content. From a pack animal Pecos tumbled the tools. In short order they had chopped sufficient pine sticks for the short fence and the gate. Before the sun sank in the west the opening giving upon the lower basin was closed against drifting cattle.

A satisfactory flat was found half-a-mile up the creek. During the evening meal and afterwards, they discussed future plans with satisfaction. There was little excitement about this home-carving, but Kirk was aware of a deep and abiding sense of gratification. He knew he would come to love this hill country range. Even now he stood ready to fight fiercely for his right to put down roots here.

Morning brought brisk and zestful activity once more. Speedily the corrals went up. Then, after the midday meal, they began to lay out the proportions of a comfortable cabin.

In early afternoon Kirk dropped his axe and

straightened as he spotted a rider advancing across the mingled sagebrush and bunch grass.

For a moment he stared. Pecos noted his motionless absorption and followed his gaze.

He grunted: "No warnin' this time. Whoever 'tis, has got a buck across the saddle bow."

Kirk's gaze did not waver. "More to it than that," he responded. "That rider's hurt! See the sag on that one side? Shoulder, I wouldn't wonder."

That the newcomer had seen them and was intentionally coming straight toward them was evident. A minute later Pecos uttered a gruff exclamation.

"That ain't no man! It's a girl! There ain't no mistakin' that thin, pinched face. By golly, she's in trouble!"

Kirk was already moving out. He had seen that the pale, blank expression of pain could not conceal evidences of striking good-looks.

They met without words. Kirk put an arresting hand on the bronc's bridle and then stepped close to this girl's knee. His practiced glance was brief and sure.

"Dislocation, eh? . . . Slip your leg over the horn. And step down—don't slide. You don't want to jar that arm. I'll see you don't fall."

Lips compressed, she complied awkwardly. He steadied her. Then she was down.

"Thanks. I—don't know whether I'd have

made it home—or not." Her voice was low, rich and strong.

He helped her to a seat on a log. Pecos stood staring as though conscious of his helplessness. Kirk indicated a canvas bucket.

"Get some cold water in that," he directed his partner. And to the girl: "I'll have to ruin the sleeve of this shirt."

She said, through clenched teeth: "Go ahead."

Carefully he cut it away. She had chestnut hair, he noted; brown eyes, a cleanly formed chin.

"This joint will have to be snapped back," he told her. "I know it hurts now—but it'll have to hurt worse before it gets any better."

She said faintly: "All right."

Pecos returned. Kirk got him, flushed and earnest of manner, to help hold the girl. He made as short work as he humanly could of the operation. There was a dull snap as the joint went back in its socket. The girl gasped, bit her lower lip sharply, then opened her eyes in surprise as he began to reduce the swelling with cold water.

"It's—done?"

"That's all there is to it," he assured her. "You'll have to rest that shoulder for a few days. It'll be pretty sore." He was drinking her in with frank admiration as he spoke. "What happened, anyway?"

"I swear I don't quite know." A ghost of a smile appeared. "I rode out after venison. It seemed I'd never find any. Then, suddenly—the buck flushed under my pony's nose. I wheeled sidewise, bringing the rifle up. I was—disgusted with myself. I hadn't seen a thing all day; then I almost rode down a deer. . . . Anyway, I let drive at a venture—"

"And hit dead center!" Kirk interposed, smiling.

"—And piled out of the saddle at the same time!" she finished ruefully. "It was the fall that did it. I—"

Pecos spoke up, gruffly. "Mind tellin' us how yuh got that buck onto yore hoss, ma'am?"

She looked at him in puzzlement. "Why, I simply did it, I suppose. I'm quite strong enough to lift a small deer with one arm."

Kirk was amazed at her grit. From his first sight of her faded but spotless Levi's and her grey, woolen shirt, and that clear-cut, courageous face, he had asked himself who she was. Remembering her bronc now, he glanced at it, saw the Ladder brand there—Cole Hutchinson's brand!

"Better let me ride home with you," Kirk proposed, when the color had returned somewhat to her face. He turned to get up his own pony.

She said: "I'm Joan Hutchinson—" as though that meant something special.

His look was level. "I'm Kirk Jordan. And this is Pecos Johnson, my partner."

"You are—expecting to build a ranch here?"

"Why not?" Pecos asked.

27

She avoided his scrutiny, but answered frankly enough: "It can come to no good."

"Yuh mean, yuh think we won't stay long?"

"I—hope you don't," she evaded. "I don't want anything to happen to you—"

"We'll stay," Pecos assured her. "And nothin'll happen to us. Rest yore mind on that."

Seeing no gain in such an exchange, yet knowing Pecos would not drop it till he chose, Kirk had gone for his pony. He came back, leading it.

"I'll toss the buck across my saddle," he said, "and then you won't have that to bother you."

"Wait," she stopped him. "Leave it, and ride my pony. That's if you'll allow me to use yours? Then when we part—"

He looked at her, wordless, at this indication that she meant not to allow him to accompany her all the way home. Then he nodded. He would take care of that in its time, he told himself.

They rode out of the basin and headed down the hills. The Ladder outfit sprawled for miles across this country. Hutchinson's headquarters buildings were far to the south, and lower down. Cole Hutchinson, Kirk realized as they neared the huge spread, had picked a site more nearly ideal for its purpose than the one on which he and Pecos had fixed, if that were possible.

Dusk overtook them. As they rode out on a rise they saw the vague shape of the buildings below.

A man's voice drifted up thinly, calling out to the stock.

Without saying anything, Joan slipped carefully down. Her voice took on a note of decision then.

"Thank you, Kirk, for what you have done for me. Had you been here longer—" She paused. "You might not have cared to. May I have my pony, please?"

"I'll ride on down with you," he offered mildly.

"No. You've done enough."

He stepped down, but made no move to exchange mounts, leaning back against her saddle. His tone was reflective: "There was a slim, dark-faced youngster. Thin lips, thin nose. Black eyes, as I remember—"

She was following his words intently. She understood at once. "Rather light-haired—?"

"Yes."

She nodded. "It was Brad Rock. One of my father's boys."

"I expected as much," he admitted.

She did not ask what Rock had had to say. Her words were suddenly urgent: "Kirk, gather your stock and drive out of this country! There can be nothing good for you here. Will you believe me?"

"Of course I do—in the way you mean. But maybe you don't know what is good for me."

"I do!" she said quickly. "At least, I know what is bad for you—for any man."

He forced a smile. "You make it out a hard land, Joan."

"No harder than it is," she insisted. "You don't know—you can't know! . . . Won't you go?"

"I'll think about it."

She took this in the way it was meant. Sadness touched her. "I have done what I could." She took the bridle of her pony with her good hand and managed to swing up. "Good-bye."

He knew better than to try to hold her. But his parting words were different: "So long."

4

Joan dismounted in the ranch yard outside the lighted kitchen and stepped to the door. "There's a buck across my pony for you," she told the cook. "Ask one of the boys to look after Boots, will you?" Then she went on through, passing the dining room, and paused in the door of the big living room.

It was low-ceilinged, but otherwise roomy. Bear and lion skins hung the walls and covered the floor. An unlit fire waited in a yawning blackened fireplace, for the weather was warm. Big, reflector-hooded hanging lamps lit the place.

A white-haired, hawk-beaked man of severe mien and commanding manner sat in a rustic chair, a sleeping hound at his feet. This was Joan's father.

"Kiddy," he greeted, in a tone which revealed deep love. "Where've you been today?"

"I've been hunting, Dad. I got a buck."

He smiled. "Where was that?"

"Up the slopes toward Geronimo Mountain."

"Meet anybody up there?" The query was guarded.

"You mean Kirk Jordan—? Yes, I met him."

He grunted. "Know his name, eh? . . . Brad

31

Rock told me about him. What's he doin' up there?"

"I believe he's decided to start a ranch."

His head reared back intolerantly, eyes glinting. "How do yuh know that?" he rasped. "See 'im buildin'?"

"There's a cabin started." She hardly knew what to say. "Dad—he seems a nice fellow. I'm sure he won't give you any trouble! Why not leave him to himself—"

"Nice? Trouble?" The echoed words were edged. "How d'yuh know all this, anyway?"

"I expect she took pains to find out," put in a heavy voice, like a half-angry insinuation.

Joan whirled. Her brother Buck, big and blocky, his blunt face sardonic, was eyeing her derisively. He had come up quietly to listen, and stood quite close. His chest was like a barrel.

Cole Hutchinson shot a keen glance at his son on reading his tone. "Never mind," he rumbled. "I reckon Joan can tell it."

Buck went on heavily, as if he hadn't heard: "Who is this Jordan, anyway? Brad Rock gave him fair warnin'! Why don't he clear out?"

"Perhaps Brad overdid it," said the girl sharply. "It would hardly be the first time for him!"

"It won't be the last, either, as long as these drifters fog in here and grab what they please!"

"He's doing you no harm!" she shot back. "He's away over on the far slope of Upper Basin!"

32

"Yeah!" Buck could be savage when he chose. "But if we let him and a few others stay, we'd soon be crowded out on the desert! What's eatin' you?" He glared. "I thought we settled all this with Eph Gowan and his kind!"

"You'll never settle anything, your way!" she told him, her eyes flashing. "All you can see is guns, violence."

"You little fool—!" Buck began.

"Stop it!" old Cole roared, with unexpected and stinging vehemence. "I don't propose to have no more of this! . . . Joan, go get ready fer supper. Buck—"

"Well, what about this Jordan, then?" Buck flung at the older man, challengingly. "Now we know he's squattin' up there. You goin' to take care of him?"

Cole blazed: "I'll take care of you, you rattle-brained whelp!"

Buck insisted pugnaciously: "And this Jordan waddy?" Then he burst out: "By God, I'll smear him plumb across the hills—finish him—if you don't do somethin' yoreself! He's had his warnin', and now you've got yours!"

For a moment, looking back from the door, her lips bloodless at this unfelial defy, Joan thought their father would suffer a stroke in his rage. Somehow he mastered himself. His lightning-darting eyes raked around and saw her standing there. His tone was taut:

"All right, Joan!" The words were peremptory. "Leave us to ourselves!"

The girl passed out of the room. So it was that she knew no more of the words which passed between father and son than did Kirk and Pecos, in their camp in the hills.

They would have remained undisturbed in any event. The deep peace of this high basin was all-pervading. The girl's veiled warning, it was true, coupled to that of the cowhand, had put Kirk on his guard.

The pair were busy again the following morning. The cabin ran up swiftly, for it was no trick to procure materials.

About midday they broke off work at an exclamation from Pecos. The little man had spied a rider who came on slowly but without pause and appeared about to pass within a quarter-mile, as though he had come down from some high shoulder of Geronimo Mountain.

Pecos and Kirk stared. The rider, passing deliberately, did the same. He was dressed in nondescript clothes, his face was dark and inscrutable.

"Apache, by gravy!" Pecos muttered tersely.

It was true. They watched for the first false move on the Indian's part, for it did not escape Kirk that this had all been Indian land at no remote period. But apparently curiosity was the Apache's chief concern. His visage was turned

34

toward the cabin till he was half-a-mile away. He passed out of sight then. Making for a rocky knoll near at hand, Pecos presently reported that he was going on without pause or change of direction—heading straight down the hills.

"What yuh s'pose that means?" he queried soberly, coming back. "Little spy work?"

"Hard to say." Kirk was undisturbed. "Eph Gowan may have wanted to know what was going on. Or the Apaches themselves may be checking up. It's my guess we'll see more or less of them in this country all the while."

They put in the remainder of the day without further disturbance. In late afternoon they saddled up and set off to circle their range, to make doubly sure the J Bar steers had no further chance to stray. What they saw pleased them no little. It only served to confirm their faith in their choice. Few cowmen in all the length and breadth of the West could boast of richer, finer range.

Returning along the barrier ridge in the soft, grey dusk, they were within a quarter-mile of the newly-built gate when Kirk jerked on the reins.

"Listen!" he commanded sharply.

A heavy chunking sound, as of the chopping of wood, came to their ears. Pecos jumped his bronc to the edge of the trees, his piercing glance raking the range beyond.

"It ain't at the cabin!" he jerked out. And then,

savagely: "But by gravy, there's men out there amongst the steers!"

Tautness caught Kirk up, carving his face lean.

"I thought so! It's Hutchinson's outfit, paying us a visit! That must be some of the bunch, knocking our gate out, while the rest are rounding up our stock. They aim to drive us out of here!"

They struck in the spurs, racing toward the gate. The sound of axes at work grew louder as they neared. Rifles came out of the scabbards under their thighs. It was Pecos who flung into an open space, threw his gun to his shoulder and blazed away.

The answer came in an instant. Fire freckled the gloom ahead; slugs whistled about them, and one glanced off Kirk's saddle horn, tearing his sleeve.

"There must be three-four down there—besides the ones hazin' the cattle down!" Pecos rifled at him, as they hauled in to take stock of the situation.

The axe-blows had ceased. Suddenly there was a rush of hoofs, and several riders spread out and charged toward them, firing as they came. Kirk and Pecos withstood that whistling blast for a moment, then were obliged to seek cover within the fringe of the pines.

Even here they were far from safe. Lead screamed off the trunks, flying about their heads. Kirk's hat sailed away, and Pecos got a slash across his cheek. Still the attackers closed in. Pecos fell back on his six-gun, for he needed all the strength of one hand to hold down his bronc.

"They'll have us on the run, here, 'fore we can write our own ticket!" he rasped harshly.

"Head out in the open!" Kirk snapped. "We'll try to flank those birds driving the steers! We've got to break that up somehow, or go under!"

They burst out of the trees on the dead run. Even in the open the blanketing darkness bade fair to defeat them. They heard an ominous rumble of hoofs, strident cries and an occasional shot. But they could see next to nothing.

"Make for the point!" Kirk grated. "We've got to head 'em and get 'em turned!"

The fleeting forms of horsemen were identified. Closing with the racing steers, Kirk and Pecos fired at these. The answer came hot and vicious.

From the trees along the ridge, the men who had attempted to cut down the pair were pouring this way now, hell for leather. Their guns crashed. Too late Kirk saw the desperateness of his position. He and Pecos were caught between two fires!

He swung out of the saddle, an arm hooked around his pony's withers. Like a dusky savage he clung to the horse, firing under its neck as he turned the animal and raced at right angles toward the head of the J Bar herd. Pecos followed his example, hunched and clinging to his mount like a leech.

Lead snarled a grisly song in that terse minute. Hutchinson punchers cried out hoarsely; but whether his and Pecos's bullets found them, or they were caught in the cross-fire of their own crowd, Kirk could not determine.

Kirk had reached the head of his steers now. Pecos was at his heels.

"Shove 'em!" Kirk called sharply.

Together they began to thrust the thundering steers inexorably toward the right. Their unceasing fire at the enemy helped.

Hutchinson's crew, those who had been detailed to stampede the herd, were pouring down the opposite side of the steers. They too exerted pressure to keep the steers from swerving. Their slugs buzzed above the tossing sea of horns like angry wasps. Pecos, receiving a graze behind the ear, was all but catapulted out of the hull. Somehow he caught himself.

Kirk was keenly aware that defeat and disaster dogged their heels. They were outnumbered by at least four to one. While it would be possible to put up a sharp resistance, the outcome would be foregone.

"We gotta get out of this, Kirk," Pecos shouted. "We're jest makin' fools of ourselves here!"

"Cut back!" he snapped bitterly.

It was either that, or be cut to pieces by the guns of the raiders.

He pivoted his bronc violently, Pecos following his example. While onrushing steers all but smashed into them, it threw the Hutchinson gunslicks past in a rush. They were not yet wholly freed from danger, however. Their maneuver had been noted. Rifles crashed in their direction. Raiders evidently detailed to rub them out wheeled back.

Then, so sharply that it was incredible, a rolling crash of gunfire broke out along the ridge. Yells echoed. There was an unearthly whoop.

"Apache devils!" Pecos bit off violently.

Kirk froze. For a second he did not know what to make of it, what could be happening. With upwards of a score of blood-thirsty savages stirred into this fight, almost anything could result. Then Kirk galvanized into action.

"Back at 'em!" he threw out sharply. "With Hutchinson's crowd and the redskins in a clash, this is our chance!"

Together they wheeled once more. They charged down the slope of the meadow at a breakneck pace. While the smash of firing seemed to rush toward them in the dark, they drew rapidly up on the drag of the J Bar herd.

Kirk was the first to divine what was happening. "The steers are turned!" he jerked out. Exultation flooded him. "They'll never hit the gate at all! . . . Jump Hutchinson's crowd! Now we can make 'em sweat for this."

Guns at the ready, they plunged forward. They were getting accustomed to this light and could see what was going on now. From the pines clothing the ridge nearly a dozen lithe, mounted figures swept down into the open, the muzzle-bursts of their fire freckling the gloom.

Hutchinson's crew had turned toward this new threat as if astounded. For a moment they were disorganized. Kirk and Pecos took advantage of the fact, pouring in a hot fire from the rear. The Apaches never ceased their sharp attack. The tables were turned with a vengeance.

Bewildered, and knowing themselves worsted, the raiders suddenly broke, turned tail and raced away in the night. Their return fire, in the face of the savage sortie of the Indians, was no more than that calculated to discourage too earnest pursuit.

But there was no pursuit. Seeing their object accomplished, the Apaches swerved off, disappeared.

"Dang queer!" Pecos grunted, scratching his stubbled chin. "They didn't make no bones about doin' us a favor!" His tone was shrewd. "Then why'd they pick up an' hightail before we had a chance to thank 'em?"

Kirk was thoughtful. "I don't know. But I'm beginning to think old Eph Gowan had something to do with this affair. The more I turn it over, the more certain I am that it just suits him to have us ranch it up here!" He was silent for a time. "It's a good thing," he added, finally, "that it suits me just as well as it does him, or I'd have something to say to that hombre that might not set so well with him!"

5

Shots echoed distantly across the hills, bearing an ominous note in the clear, limpid evening quiet. Kirk Jordan jerked the skillet back off the coals in the stone fireplace and in three swift strides reached the cabin door.

Pecos was hustling up from the corrals, trouble in his lean, sober face.

"Where was that?" Kirk threw at him.

"Come from off that way." The gnarled little man pointed across the rolling basin. "Sounded like trouble."

Without more words, each grabbed up a rifle and made for a point from which they could overlook the spread of the basin.

"Bunch of riders foggin' it over there!" Pecos whipped out. "Two, three—four, I count; one a good ways in the lead!"

"Those birds are houndin' that hombre in the lead!" Kirk burst out. "Three to one—and they'll soon overhaul him, too!"

"He's pretty near dead beat! Reckon this 's some more o' them damned Hutchinson tricks!"

Soon they were on their broncs and striking at an angle calculated to intercept the chase.

If the fugitive was aware of the existence in this wilderness basin of a ranch which might spell sanctuary, he failed to reveal that knowledge in his actions. His present course would carry him well beyond the J Bar limits.

Pecos, seeing this, straightened in his stirrups, placed a horny palm alongside his mouth, and loosed a stentorian bellow.

"Hey, there!" And a moment later: "Over this way! Swing over!" He waved wildly.

"He sees us," Kirk flung at him tersely. "He's coming over."

"Jest in time!" Pecos exulted fiercely. "That bronc's on 'is last legs, shore!" Then his eyes fixed piercingly. "By Godfrey, Kirk—I was right! Them's Hutchinson's wolves, doin' the chasin'! I dang near smoked that feller in the lead, the other night!"

"You get another chance now!" Kirk gritted. "I don't know what this is all about, but we'll take a hand to the extent of finding out!"

He threw up his rifle and flung a slug which knocked up dust under the nose of one of the pursuers' horses. Pecos followed his lead. Nor did they slack their pace, hammering forward as if they invited a head-on clash.

The fugitive, yelling unintelligently, swung aside out of the line of fire. The Hutchinson punchers, whether surprised or chagrined, suddenly broke to one side, and almost with the concerted flight of swallows, swung behind a protecting rock dyke.

A moment later they answered with a hot fire.

Pecos and Kirk took cover and pumped a couple of searching shots amongst the rocks.

The saddle carbines in the hands of the Hutchinson punchers were no match for rifles. They started to pull away, yelling defiance and raining curses.

The man they had thought to ride down came racing back now, an ugly rage in his face.

"Take after 'em!" he bawled. "Them skunks would've killed me without battin' an eye! Smoke 'em down!"

Kirk sharply hauled his bronc up across this man's path.

"Hold on," he bit off, impellingly. "We got you out of that jackpot! Suppose you cool down a bit!"

"Dammit, man, they was after my hide, I tell yuh!" the other flamed truculently.

"That's no reason to go off half-cocked. Suppose you give us an idea what this 's all about, first."

Pecos took a careful look at the man. He was about Kirk's age, and had the look of a drifting puncher. Rips and tears showed here and there in his clothes. He was cooling rapidly after his quick anger, but something like a sinister shade still hung over his lean, hatchet-like face.

"Wal!" Pecos barked, with his usual gruffness. "Who are yuh?"

"Parsons is my handle," was the ready reply. "Folks call me Slim. . . . Reckon I 'pologize fer shootin' off my lip a minute ago," he added, addressing Kirk frankly. "I was pretty riled."

Kirk's smile was tight. "Reckon you was. We won't hold that against you. But we're still waitin' to hear what this was all about."

Slim Parsons stepped down from his worn and lathered pony. He turned to them both, then, with great simplicity.

"Why, shore! Reckon it's soon told. . . . I been ridin' fer a couple seasons back fer the Cross Hatch, thirty miles or so south in the breaks. Old Hoke Mellon's spread. Things are goin' to the bad with Hoke, an' he dunno jest what to do 'bout it. . . ."

"What yuh mean, goin' to the bad?" Pecos interposed.

"Wal—the Cross Hatch herd's thinnin' out, fer one thing. An' the range ain't what it used to be, no more."

"Ahuh! Yuh mean Mellon's gettin' crowded out?"

"Reckon that's what it amounts to. Anyhow, he let me an' a couple other boys go last week."

"Whyn't yuh clear out, then?" Pecos asked, gruffly.

"The other boys headed south fer the Gavilan. They wanted me to go 'long. I said no. Decided I'd strike west into Arizona. So I worked north a ways so's to hit the passes when I swung into the hills."

"Ahuh! An' what about Hutchinson's lobos, then?"

"Wal—" Parsons appeared to fumble for his words. "The Cross Hatch never had no out-an'-out scrapes with the Ladder. I never suspected I was runnin' into a hornet's nest!" He insisted on this stoutly, as though it might be called into question. "Seein' I'd be ridin' the grub line a while, I reckoned I'd make that my first stopover."

Wrinkles of dawning amusement appeared around Pecos's eyes. "So yuh got into a wrangle in the Ladder bunkhouse, said too much, an' they chased yuh out, huh?"

"Said, hell!" Parsons flared, wrath mantling his bony cheeks afresh. "I never got no chance to open my face!"

"You mean they ordered you off the place?" Kirk put in.

"Not that either! By gravy, somebody must've recognized me comin'! I got along okay, without even a warnin', till I started to jog into the Ladder ranch yard. Then, real sudden, some damn fool whipped out a six-gun an' blazed away at me, swearin' a blue streak—I reckon that was Buck Hutchinson, blast his ornery black hide!"

"I'll be damned!" Pecos breathed, his jaw dropping.

Parsons jerked his head in confirmation. "That's exactly what happened! Only they didn't let it go at that. Natcherally, I hightailed out of there in a hurry. I heard Buck yellin' to some of his boys. A few minutes later I seen 'em doggin' me. I knowed I didn't have no chance in the open—my bronc was fagged already. I was 'bout ready to hole up in the rocks an' make a hard endin' of it, when yuh showed up."

"You got a rotten deal, all right, Parsons," Kirk said. "Come over to the spread. We'll put you up."

Pecos was not so readily satisfied about what had happened. He asked Slim Parsons dozens of questions, and to an extent sympathized with him. Kirk, who remained wary of the drifting cowboy for some reason he could scarcely name, did not know whether his partner's interest was designed or not. Pecos was deep. He might be simulating accord with the newcomer for reasons of his own.

At any rate, the way the two stuck together that evening, endlessly talking, discussing the Ladder outfit and Cole Hutchinson's range monopoly, went definitely against Kirk. When Parsons expressed an interest in the little J Bar layout, and Pecos began to explain for him something of their hopes and aims, Kirk felt sure his partner was going too far.

Parsons did not drift on when morning came,

although Pecos, making a swift survey, reported no Hutchinson hands hovering about the basin. That was all right. The grub-liner's bronc was in bad case; a day's rest was the horse's due, and Kirk would have denied it to no man not an enemy.

He approved too, Slim's willingness to catch up a J Bar bronc and turn to help with the ranch work.

After supper that evening, Parsons accosted Kirk. Kirk expected the other to announce that he was drifting on in the morning. Instead, Parsons opened up:

"Jordan, looks to me like yuh got plenty of work here to keep 'nother man besides yoreselves busy. I was aimin' to drift on over the mountain, but I like the looks of things here; an' I owe you somethin' too. How 'bout it. Got room fer an extra hand?"

Somehow, Kirk was not surprised to have him ask for a job. His answer came slowly, for Pecos was listening.

"I haven't got the whole say, Parsons. But for my part, I say no—"

"Hell, Kirk!" Pecos struck in. "We can use 'nother man, an' yuh know it."

Kirk refused to meet his eye. He spent all his attention on Parsons, whose face fell with manifest disappointment.

"Reckon I wouldn't want to join on against

yore say-so, Jordan, even if I could," he admitted, with a show of candor. "But I shore think yo're makin' a mistake. From what Pecos tells me, Hutchinson's hell bent on drivin' yuh out of the basin. Two men wouldn't stand a chance against him—"

"Slim here's got plenty uh reason to hate Cole Hutchinson, too!" Pecos urged, watching Kirk's stern face in a puzzled way. "What's eatin' yuh, Kirk? He's a man made to order fer us!"

Kirk conceded as much. When all was said and done, some hidden instinct deep in his core told him the whole situation had fallen out too patly. Besides he had not liked Parsons's face from the beginning.

He shook his head.

"Sorry, Parsons. I ain't sayin' I got anything against you, personally. But it takes money to hire punchers, and to be plain about it, money's something we haven't got any too much of if we're going to pull through till the first beef-cut."

That there was sound sense in this even Pecos could not gainsay. He swallowed plain disappointment, nodding gloomily; loyal to Kirk's decision even when he believed him to be in the wrong. For Parsons's part, he started to say something quickly, then checked himself.

Kirk believed he caught that thought. Parsons had been about to offer to ride for the J Bar for nothing, for a time; he caught it back in the nick of time, as he believed, realizing that it would only too plainly reveal his eagerness to ride for the brand.

And why was he so eager to do that? Kirk asked himself the question soberly. He was too experienced to snap at the first handy explanation—that this was a plot, and Buck Hutchinson had hoped to plant a treacherous spy on them in this manner. Kirk had no proof of that. Nor, he reflected grimly, had he any proof that it was not the case.

With the first streaks of dawn, Parsons rolled out with Kirk and Pecos, downed his breakfast in silence, mumbled "So long—an' much obliged," in a grudging way, and a few minutes later jogged away from the ranch.

In a few hours Slim Parsons was forgotten—at least until he was remembered suddenly and jarringly, late the next day.

6

They had discovered a break in the barrier ridge, high in one corner of their spacious grazing meadow, through which J Bar steers were finding their way to stray out into the basin. Pecos reported it first; he had seen a couple of their steers where none ought to be, and it laid on them the wary suspicion that rustling might be Hutchinson's answer to his defeat at the hands of the Apaches.

Then Kirk discovered the break in their boundary, and they grew easier.

"Suits me to have it turn out like this," Pecos grinned, his seamed face breaking into a thousand lines and creases. "Fer once I'm duckin' trouble. Reckon I never expected to change that much! . . . But if a bunch of rustlers who knowed this country was to git into us, they'd soon wipe us out."

Kirk assented soberly. He was not deceived as to the extent of the chance they were taking.

"It wouldn't have been a bad idea to have ridden over to Cole Hutchinson's Ladder spread, first chance I had, and spoke my little piece. The little fellows always rile a big rancher when they crowd in close. It's too late now, of course. But it might have saved us trouble in the end."

Pecos opened his eyes in an expression of disbelief. He was familiar with his partner's attitude toward the large ranchers.

"That shore don't sound like you!" he blurted. And then, as a new thought struck him: "But I reckon there's things about this set-up that make it different from the usual, huh?" And he watched Kirk shrewdly.

If Kirk was conscious of his reference to the girl, he did not show it.

"I'm figuring a lot of things different these days. This ranch is no experiment with me. It's got to stick! And any means I can hit on that'll bring that end about is good enough for me."

"Uh-huh," Pecos grunted. He could find nothing of importance to add to that. "Wal, let's get this leak plugged up."

It was routine work. They jogged away from the cabin at midday and an hour later were on the spot.

"I expect there's a few head drifted through and grazing down the slope," Kirk remarked. "I'll cut a circle down and haze 'em back, while you start cutting posts for the break."

Pecos assented, swinging out of the saddle and unlimbering the axe. He started for the nearby scrub, while Kirk jogged out of sight.

For half-an-hour the gnarled little man worked steadily. He had enough to think about, and it was not until a crashing in the brush some ways away attracted his attention that he so much as lifted his head.

Beyond the pine openings and rocky humps, cluttered with brush, he spotted Kirk driving six or seven steers this way. For a few moments he watched, eyes squinted—then he grinned, as one of the fractious steers broke aside in a wild, lumbering attempt to get away. Kirk went hammering after the animal.

Without any hint of warning, the quiet afternoon split to the rhythmic *spang* of a rifle shot.

Pecos jerked stiffly erect. All humor ran out of his cheeks as they went taut.

In mid-stride, Kirk's pony did a cartwheel. Horse and rider flew through the air and landed asprawl, sliding to a stop amidst clouds of dust.

"God!" Pecos jerked out.

The axe flew from his grasp. The next second, rifle in hand, he was making in great strides for the spot, several hundred yards distant, where Kirk lay.

The latter sat up dazedly as Pecos reached him.

"Are yuh bad hurt, Kirk? Anythin' broke?" Keenest anxiety spoke in that hoarse tone.

Kirk shook his head, as much to clear it of fog as to indicate a negative.

"Don't think—so. I sure stretched a link or two, though!" And Kirk grinned with tight-pinched lips.

Pecos didn't catch that. Once he had got the

other's terse headshake, he turned his attention to their surroundings, a sharp vigilance on him.

They were in a small brush-protected hollow. Beside them stretched the carcass of the bronc for extra cover had they needed it. It was dead. A slackening rill of blood curled from the hole drilled in its chest. Kirk's amazed, indignant eyes took that in, then he growled:

"That's plain talk! But I don't even know where it came from. Lightning doesn't strike swifter!"

Pecos completed his inspection of the near terrain. He turned back, a frown knitting his brow.

"Can't see a dang thing," he admitted.

"Hear anything while you were getting here?"

"No—Hold on, mebby I did hear hoofs or suthin'. I was plumb worried 'bout whether I'd find yuh with a hole in yore gizzard, an' was bent on settlin' that question first."

Kirk didn't blame him.

"There's times when you simply have to miss something. But what you heard must've been that bushwhacker doing his sneak."

Nevertheless they were wary of taking chances when they straightened and set about more thoroughly combing the adjacent territory. Rifles at the ready, each went a different way. It was half-an-hour before Pecos called gruffly from a spot on the rough ground over west. Kirk went to him.

"Here's where he stopped," said the little man. "Never got down off his bronc at all. He was doggin' yuh—waitin' fer just such a chance. He let fly an' hightailed."

Kirk's first thought had been that it was a Ladder gunman. It was difficult to conceive of the father of Joan Hutchinson resorting to such tactics; but what else was he to believe?

Earlier in the day he had still privately entertained some hope of striking a balance with the big ranch owner, once they met under favorable circumstances. But now any such intention was automatically abandoned.

"It's each man for himself in this!" he told himself grimly. "Let Hutchinson look out for himself. I'll undertake to do the same."

He might have let the matter drop there for the time being, but not so Pecos. The latter ran back to where he had ground-anchored his bronc, swung aboard and returned to where they had found the tracks of the assassin's horse.

"Back in just a minute," he called to Kirk, who was engaged in releasing his saddle from the shot pony.

Kirk frowned, but made no reply. He was unprepared for his partner's return, ten minutes later, with a grave expression of countenance, and carrying something in his hand that looked like a torn rag.

"What have you got there?"

55

"Bandana," Pecos returned, tersely. "Our bush-whackin' friend lost it in his hurry." He held it up.

Kirk stared. It was a kerchief of a peculiar pattern, more faded purple and green than red—and it was either the same one, or one strikingly similar, to one they had noted the day before around the stringy throat of the drifter, Slim Parsons.

Kirk said, oddly: "That—that looks—"

"I know." Pecos's nod was curt, but his glance was direct, without evasion. "Kinda seems like I made a mistake, huh?"

"Either you did then, or we're both making one now. Parsons *was* wearing a bandana like that, wasn't he?"

"Yeh. It's his orright."

"So that settles that. There's not much doubt about that hombre's intentions. The next question is—who sent him?"

"Pretty plain—now. Ain't it?"

"I wouldn't be too sure." Kirk knotted his forehead over the problem. "A lot depends on the motive for knocking me off."

It was all plain as a cattle trail in wet mud to Pecos. "Dang it, Kirk! There ain't but one outfit wants yore hide nailed to the corral fence. Don't go lettin' yore hopes warp yore good sense!"

Kirk was unmoved by this warning.

"If Parsons hoped mainly for a chance to knock

me off, when he came here, why go through all the red tape—getting himself chased, being rescued, fishing for a job? If he had any such intentions, he could have made a job of it without ever showing himself to us."

"That's so—" Pecos admitted, thoughtfully. "But mebby that wasn't his first scheme. Mebbe it made him mad at yuh when yuh seen through him."

"Maybe."

There was a reserve in Kirk's agreement which roweled Pecos. "Wal—then who'n Tophet do yuh reckon wanted a man on the J Bar, if not Hutchinson?" he demanded testily.

"There's Eph Gowan."

"Gowan?" Pecos's stare was blank.

"Pecos, Gowan hates Hutchinson like a cow hates a rattler! He'd go to any length to smash him. Think back—how he gave in about the water; directed us up here, even offered help! It's all plain reading."

"I reckon it is, looked at that way."

"Our trouble lies in the fact that we don't know this range," Kirk proceeded. "You can't tell enough about a man, sometimes, by his outside. Is this Parsons what he says he is? I say no! He's a gun ready for anybody's hire. It would have been possible for Gowan to make a deal with him—send him up here to join on with us."

"But them Ladder waddies?"

"Parsons could have scraped a quarrel with them, seen to it that they chased him this way. Eph Gowan may even have hatched that scheme. I'm beginning to find him deeper and deeper!"

"Shore. But wantin' yuh dead would be his last aim," Pecos maintained stoutly.

"True. But you know Parsons's kind. I turned him away. It may have burned him up, and he decided to get even."

Pecos carried Kirk's saddle back to the ranch, and presently returned with a fresh bronc. They resumed their work, keeping a watchful eye peeled now, but meeting with no further disturbance. It was plain they both had been thinking matters over, for after supper that evening Pecos queried:

"Wal, what'll yuh do, Kirk?"

"I've a good mind to fog down and brace Gowan with a few pointed questions."

"Won't do no good."

"Not unless I read between the answers," Kirk admitted. "I can at least try that."

"Meanwhile, if that coyote, Parsons, came back once I reckon we can count on seein' him again, huh?"

It was his partner's way of warning Kirk that he must be on his guard unremittingly. Kirk got it. It did not impress him unduly.

Accordingly, the following day he got up a bronc, swung into the hull and jogged away down the slopes. He rode leisurely, for he was keeping a strict watch about him. Moreover, he wanted to turn things over in his mind before he tackled Gowan.

It was a beautiful day. The advanced season had not taken all the green freshness out of the sagebrush and the trees; but the lower he got, Kirk noted a brown dust coating everything slightly. Faint whisps of it curled away on the vagrant breeze.

"Dust!" he grunted. "Never really took note of that before. It means the storms around here are pretty severe, all right."

His mind returned to other matters, then. He kept for the most part to cover; and though he was on the lookout for any animate thing around him, it is likely he would have passed the spot by had it not been for the sudden shying of his bronc.

Kirk pulled in. Seeing nothing, he had to move back a few feet, from where he could catch a glimpse through the interstices of the brush. Suddenly his breath went out of him in a gasp.

"Good gravy!"

There was a dead man there, sprawled in the dust. It was a puncher. He lay half on his face; but after one keen glance Kirk made reasonably sure he knew who it was. His face drew into thin, stern lines.

He got down, tossing the reins over to hold his

pony, and moved forward. Slim Parsons lay cold and long dead. The tracks of coyotes circled the spot; but there was enough left of him to tell a lot.

Parsons had died by no gunshot. The only marks Kirk found on him were those by a knife, but there were plenty of those.

"Huh!"

The answer came to Kirk in a flash. Apache work!

He stood up and looked around. He was utterly alone at the spot with the corpse now. Either tell-tale sign had been smoothed out, or none had been left, for only the gouged tracks of Parsons's missing horse, and the man's own body, remained.

"Makes things doubly plain," Kirk murmured. "Only Indians would or could do a job like that!"

He returned to his bronc, and swinging into the saddle, sat quietly while he rolled a smoke and lit it. This discovery put a different face on things; and when he moved on, he no longer rode in the direction of Eph Gowan's basin below in the desert. It would do no good.

"Gowan never sent that drifter to us," he was convinced. "If he had, it would have been a case of hands-off for his Apaches. Somehow they found out Parsons's intentions toward us—maybe saw him have his chance at me, from some high point. One of 'em took care of the rest.

"It wasn't," he reiterated, thinking carefully, "Gowan who shoved Parsons our way at all. . . . That kind of puts it up to Cole Hutchinson, and no mistake!"

7

The sun rose red and sullen this morning in a coppery sky. It seemed in accord with the mood which hung over the little J Bar spread in the basin. Several days had passed since Hutchinson's raiders had successfully attempted to drive them out of the country. The cabin was finished. Everything was in order now, with only minor tasks to be completed. No further trouble had sought Kirk and Pecos out. Yet daily they waited for Hutchinson's next move.

Pecos came to the door of the cabin and there paused, to scan the heavens shrewdly.

"I reckon Gowan wasn't far wide of the mark," he commented, a note of apprehension in his words. "Looks like this country can put on a real storm when it gets started."

"Yeh." Kirk, at his shoulder, scanned the horizon with practiced eye. "There's wind in that sky. A sand storm must be hitting the desert."

" 'S all right, long's it don't come up here."

It was Kirk who, half-an-hour later, came back from the creek with some knotty problem showing plainly in his face.

"What's up?" Pecos queried.

"The creek water is slacking off—"

Pecos bristled. He read instantly what was in his partner's mind.

"If that's the case, we better be lookin' into this! There ain't nothin' in this layout more important to us than our water." He swung the cartridge-belt of his six-gun around his waist, and buckling it on, started for the corrals.

They saddled up speedily. Pecos started to swing into the hull, then paused.

"Yuh don't s'pose this is a trick to toll us both away from the basin?" he demanded anxiously.

Kirk thought it over dispassionately. "I don't believe so," he decided finally. "It's a chance we've got to take—unless you think you'd better stay here while I go up the creek!"

Pecos grunted grimly: "Not by a damn sight! We're both ridin'!"

With a tight-lipped, mirthless smile, Kirk swung his bronc away. They rode up the meadow. The ground rose steadily toward the massive bulge of Geronimo Mountain. The headwaters of Feather Creek were high and hidden.

As they crossed a hog-back, Kirk suddenly drew in with a jerk.

"Listen!"

But Pecos's face, too, was keen and intent. From somewhere farther up the mountain, perhaps a mile away, perhaps several, there came down the ringing, shattered echo of a rifle-shot. Beneath it they seemed to catch the sullen, broken mutter of six-gun fire. Then silence returned, ominous and blanketing.

"That's from up the crick, shore's fate!" Pecos burst out tensely. "There's a fight goin' on up there!"

Kirk found no choice but to agree. Though they had wasted no time before, they pushed forward at the double now.

Then the creek wormed out of a gorge-like canyon. It looked like they would have to abandon the horses if they followed it further. The grizzled little man gave vent to an ejaculation.

"By gravy, there's a fork up here, Kirk!"

The latter had already noted as much. At the mouth of the canyon the creek divided and one branch, as near as could be determined, ran off to the south to lead a course separated by many miles from Feather Creek.

"Here's where they'd set to work, if Hutchinson's outfit was figurin' on doin' any divertin'," Pecos proceeded.

Kirk had already seen this. They rode forward warily. Then Pecos, ranging to one side, swore tensely.

"The ground's plumb ripped up by hoofs over here!" he got out guardedly. "But I don't see nothin' else. What's it mean?"

Still siding the creek, Kirk pulled up beside the fork. His face was curiously bleak as his gaze ran over the spot.

"Here it is!" he called. "Somebody started a rock fill to cut off Feather Creek and throw the water the other way. They didn't get very far—and the natural current took care of the rest!"

Pecos's visage was blank. "Why'd they stop?" he wanted to know. "There's not much question about it bein' the Ladder bunch, aimin' to freeze us out on the water end. Why'd they knock off in the middle of it?"

"The Apaches may have stepped in again," Kirk thought. "I can't see where all their generosity comes in—but I can't see any other answer either."

"Some unshod hoof-prints around," Pecos pointed out. "That looks like Injun work, all right."

The great problem remained—what had happened? They started to quarter the spot minutely, searching for clues. It was Kirk who yanked his bronc to a trembling halt at the edge of a thick stand of lodge pole pines a hundred yards from the fork.

"What did yuh find?" Pecos called.

Kirk neglected to answer, sitting his saddle as if frozen there. The little man ranged up alongside of him. Then he, too, froze to immobility, his eyes staring.

Before them, dangling from a rope run over a high limb, hung a lifeless Apache, his head twisted awry.

"Good God!" Pecos jerked out, hoarsely.

Kirk slid out of the saddle, fishing a knife from his pocket as he did so. In a trice he had the Indian down. Though the latter had been hung only a matter of minutes, there was no hope of reviving him. His neck had been broken.

Making sure of this, Kirk lifted the limp form in his arms. It was a matter of both strength and ingenuity to reach his saddle with this burden. Somehow he managed it, the Indian stretched across his thighs.

"What yuh goin' to do with 'im?" Pecos queried.

"Little enough I can do. I'll take him down to Eph Gowan's place. The Indians would have taken him themselves, but there's not much doubt the fight here was pretty hot." He pointed to dark splotches on the ground which appeared to be blood. "Hutchinson's crowd wasn't outnumbered much, or they'd have had no time for this hanging. Likely the other Apaches trailed them for revenge."

Pecos shrugged. "Not much we can do 'bout it. We don't even know what direction they took."

After making sure that Feather Creek was not seriously obstructed, they turned down the long slopes. The burnished, reddish cast to the sky had deepened. It carried almost the effect of a strange, unseasonable sunset. The sun itself was a swimming molten ball, faintly obscured. The atmosphere was heavy.

"You better stick here," Kirk proposed, when they neared the ranch. "No much chance of Hutchinson's lobos turning up, but it's no harm done to make sure."

Pecos nodded. "I'll be ready for 'em," was his terse promise.

Kirk passed through the gate, which had been rebuilt, and jogged on down the hills. It was a long ride, but he had plenty to think over.

He was appalled by the lurid aspect of the sky as he rode out into the lower basin and headed for Gowan's place. At no time had he seen so much as a distant rider. But there were half-a-dozen shaggy, saddleless ponies in Gowan's corral.

He rode past, and as he drew up before the house, several Apaches appeared, to stare at him steadily. He gave them the once-over. Straight Tongue was standing in the door.

"What you got dere?" he queried colorlessly.

Kirk explained quietly about the water of Feather Creek slacking off, and how he had ridden up the hills with Pecos and what they had found there.

"I brought him down to you," he ended simply.

Something unnamable burned in the fierce eyes of these voiceless braves. But it was not directed against Kirk. Two of their number helped him lift the dead Apache down from the saddle. They carried the body out of sight around the house. Kirk turned to interrogate Straight Tongue.

"Where's Gowan?"

The Indian eyed him inscrutably for so long that Kirk thought he did not mean to answer at all. The words came deliberately: "Jordan, we t'ank you for what you done. We no forget. Apache not like brudder hang. Poison."

"That's all right, Straight Tongue. If I had been twenty minutes sooner, I might have prevented it. . . . And Gowan?"

Eph appeared in the door at this moment. He seemed elaborately casual, yet darted a questioning scrutiny at Kirk. Kirk opened up without preamble.

"Gowan, did you know what we were headin' into up in the hills?"

Eph became wary. "I dunno what yuh mean! I told yuh the story, Jordan. Why?"

Kirk bored him steadily. "You didn't figure on our pulling chestnuts out of the fire for you when you told us about that upper range?" His tone was strict, but not accusing.

Gowan went mahogany-colored. He controlled himself with an effort.

"I'll answer you with 'nother question," he growled. "Jordan, if you'd seen that range, without ever talkin' to me, would you've settled onto it anyway?"

Kirk forced a grin. "I expect I would—"

"Then you can thank yore stars yuh did see me first—an' I saw you!" The long teeth snapped. "If I hadn't decided you'd do to stick, do yuh think you'd be there now?"

Kirk had not missed this side of the situation. He nodded slowly. "We're obliged to you, Gowan. That's clear. It's just that I've got a dislike of being misled about anything."

"Uh-huh. Reckon yuh got a right to be." Eph dropped the subject easily. "Yuh done the right thing, Jordan—bringin' that Apache in. Good thing yuh thought to do it!"

Kirk passed this over in his turn. "The Indians have done plenty for us. . . . I'll be heading back up the hills, I guess." His eye went to the sky, deepening in tone now to the color of a dust-pall.

"Hold on!" Gowan was urgent. "How 'bout tellin' me what's goin' on up there?"

Kirk told briefly what the last few days had brought. It was impossible to sate Gowan's curiosity, but finally Kirk turned away. Some of the Indians had returned by now. They stood around, glancing at him, but without speaking. He knew they felt that he understood them.

"This looks pretty bad!" Gowan called, his own glance raking the heavens. "Yuh better stay till it's over, Jordan!"

"No—I'll make it back where I can watch things."

69

Kirk thought he had time enough; but he had scarcely reached the first rises of the lower basin when the wind moaned and sand began rustling around him. It grew hotter by the minute, and the air was stifling.

The storm increased momentarily. He pulled off his kerchief, knotted it over his nostrils. The bronc he could do nothing for. He could only hope that when he got within the trees, the suffocating dust would not be so bad.

But it began to appear that he had made a grave mistake in leaving Gowan's place after all. In a matter of minutes he found it all but impossible to tell where he was heading.

"Bad!" he told himself, soberly. "I can well believe Gowan's story of how the grass died! It looks like more of it has got a good chance of dying, in this—"

He broke off his thinking sharply as he glimpsed some moving form through the swirling murk ahead. Was it the wind, swaying the cedar clumps? Even as the possibility rose to the surface of his mind, he knew better.

There was someone else, mounted on a bronc and wandering almost aimlessly before the storm, as he was doing, just ahead. Was it Pecos, searching for him; or one of the Apaches, or—his heart chilled. Was it a Hutchinson puncher? If this was the case, he had a fight on his hands. . . .

70

He strained his eyes, without seeing anything. Then he got another glimpse. It was Joan Hutchinson, alone, wandering in the blinding storm, perhaps lost!

8

"Joan!" Kirk cried. "What are you doing out in this?"

They came close together. The girl peered as if making sure of him.

"Kirk! Is it you?" She had to raise her voice. "You're miles from your cabin."

"And you're a long ways from home," he retorted, watching her out of reddened eyes. "Do you know in what direction it lies?"

She seemed to listen for a moment, then her gaze widened. "I'm not lost!" she exclaimed; "if that's what you're thinking."

"That's exactly what you are," he declared. "I'll see you home."

She resisted momentarily, riding at his knee. Plainly she did not relish the idea of being led to safety. "Kirk! You can't go down to the Ladder Ranch—!"

He was brusque: "Why not?"

"Your life isn't safe!"

He brushed that aside. "It's your life I'm thinking of."

She would have protested, but at his tone she refrained.

They started off. It was hard going. Kirk had to fight the constant tendency of his pony to turn tail to the blast.

A time came when the ponies staggered, as if all their strength were needed to remain upright against the force of the storm. Kirk knew it could not go on much longer. They must either soon come to the Hutchinson ranch, or abandon the horses to their fate, and, on foot, stagger ahead perhaps to a destiny no less grim. He thrust his face toward Joan, managed to make his hoarse words heard:

"I know we're headed right! Do you know how much farther it is—have you any idea where we are?"

"No-no—" she faltered. "Go on, Kirk. We can't stop here!"

There was a plea in her voice that stirred his pulse, set it pounding in a warm surge. He loved this girl.

It was a strange moment for him, not untouched with grimness. He had no guarantee that he would succeed in his object. There was an ironic note in the circumstance that he should discover his love for Joan at a time when it was far from impossible that he should lose her forever.

Their release came suddenly. They were fighting their way across an open flat, the storm enclosing them so effectually that they might have been a dozen miles from any slightest landmark. Then suddenly a shadow rose at their side. The girl peered, leaned to peer again—and uttered a cry.

73

"The corral fence, Kirk!"

Kirk pushed over, saw that she was right. They had paralleled the fence for several yards, apparently; they might have missed it altogether. But now Joan knew where they were. Safety lay within hand's reach.

Even so, she did not immediately move. Sitting her saddle like a statue, she fought out an inner struggle, answered a question which would have made Kirk's lips twitch in spite of himself had he known. She wanted him to leave her here. Her deepest instinct was to send him away, so that her father or Buck Hutchinson should never know what he had done. Buck had already divined her attitude toward this rangy, quiet-voiced man; to have it confirmed would sting her brother to unpredictable violence.

But she dared not send Kirk away. It would be an act of the most cold-hearted selfishness to turn him back into this. With the distance he had to go to reach his little spread in the Upper Basin, his chances were probably better here, whatever the issue.

As if he understood what she was going through, Kirk gave her her moment. She turned to him.

"Kirk, I did need your help! I don't know how to thank you, but I shall try. . . . Come."

They dismounted at a corner of the house. Here a number of ponies stood, head down, in the meager protection of a slackening eddy. They left their mounts with the others. Kirk supported the girl by an arm as they staggered around the corner toward the door.

"You must come in," she told him, looking up.

He sensed something in her tone that made him hesitate. "If you'd rather I didn't—"

"What could you do?" she demanded. "You will have to get your breath!"

He said no more. He wanted to lay eyes on Cole Hutchinson in any event; had some time ago considered riding down here boldly with that end in view. Had it not been for today's happenings, he would have done so eventually.

The house was dark, for no lights had been lit. But they presently became accustomed to this.

"Shake out your dust," Joan proposed, with an attempt at lightness; "then watch that you don't lift your feet too high!"

"It does weigh me down," he admitted.

He was busy slapping the sand out of his shirt and kerchief and up-tilting his gun holster, when there walked into the room a broad, stocky man of about his own age. Kirk had no idea who it might be. But the other was plainly at home here, his manner as heavy as his features.

"What's up?" he flung carelessly at Joan, all the while scrutinizing Kirk narrowly.

The girl controlled her agitation to a kind of stiffness. "Buck, this is Kirk Jordan—"

"What!" His deep-chested rasp cut across her words. He shot Kirk a glare of defiance that would have stung another to anger. "You're the hombre that's runnin' stock up in the hills, eh?"

Kirk's face was frozen. He nodded shortly. "In the face of some unusual difficulty," he responded dryly, "I manage to do that."

He guessed now who this fellow was, even though the man did not resemble Joan.

Buck's visage had gone the shade of mahogany.

"Jordan," he grated; "you've been warned to clear out of this country!"

Kirk nodded curtly. It seemed scarcely worth his while to retort. But Joan came swiftly to his support:

"Buck!" she exclaimed. "Kirk brought me home through this storm when I might not have made it myself! I asked him to come in—"

"Well," Buck's jarring retort came swiftly— "that saves me the trouble of huntin' him up, at any rate!"

The girl was arrested by his tone. "What are you going to do?" she asked, straining for calm.

"I'm goin' to kick him off this range! And if that don't stick, I'll finish him!"

Running his eye over the other's brawn, Kirk had to admit that physically, at least, Buck Hutchinson should be able to do either of these things. But he gave no sign of his contempt.

"I expect I'm out of place, Hutchinson—

feeling the way you do," he said quietly. "I'll go."

Buck flared up: "You're damned right you'll go! And you'll go far and fast!"

Kirk arrested, averse to being pushed. He surveyed Buck coolly. "So?" he countered softly.

"I don't like yore tone, Jordan!" Buck jerked out. "Joan, stand away from him!"

It was as much a threat as an order. The girl made a quick movement, but it was to put herself between the two men, her back to Kirk.

"Leave your gun where it is!" she told Buck sharply. "I know perfectly what you are thinking of! You won't do it!"

"Stand aside!" he bellowed. His face was rock-hard now, a vein pulsing in his leathery cheek.

Just then a heavy step sounded and an authoritative voice demanded: "What's this?"

"Joan's brought that damned squatter down here," Buck raged, without turning.

Kirk's eyes went to the newcomer. He knew in a flash that this blocky, commanding man must be Cole Hutchinson. The rancher strode forward deliberately.

"What are you doin' here?" he rapped out at Kirk, suddenly.

Joan would have spoken up, but Kirk was ahead of her. "I met your daughter in the storm and brought her home."

Some rigidity went out of Cole.

Buck broke in truculently: "What was he doin' on our range? By God, I'll put an end to this—!"

"Hold on!" Cole thundered harshly. "You won't do nothin'." He faced Kirk. "I'm obliged to yuh, Jordan. That's all I can say. . . . What's this about yore ranchin' on my upper range?"

Kirk spoke levelly. "I know nothing about your range. I'm a dozen miles from here—in the high basin. Why did you try to break down my gates and drive my stock off? Was there anything to gain in trying to divert Feather Creek?"

Cole stood immobile, his eyes opaque. The silence was long. Finally the old man said: "You were warned away from Ladder country. Such things happen. . . . Joan, show this man out."

The girl caught her breath. Her cheeks burned at the shortness of it. But she was glad enough to see Kirk go clear; her glance asked him for understanding.

Kirk remained where he was for a long moment, studying Cole Hutchinson; trying to fathom what manner of man this was. Then he nodded shortly. "I'm leaving, Hutchinson." He swung on his heel, and ignoring Buck, followed Joan to the door and out.

Cole watched their departure, waiting until he heard the outer door swing. Then he whirled on Buck. His features were knotted, his jaw thrust out.

"Breakin' down gates an' drivin' stock, eh?

Divertin' water, by God! So that's how half-a-dozen of my boys came to get shot up! . . . An' yuh told me they got into a scrape in Hazen's saloon at the Crossin'!"

Buck flared: "What if I did? We've got to get rid of that hombre, whether you see it or not!"

"We?" the older man echoed savagely. "I'll have you know I'm still runnin' the Ladder!"

Buck started for an inner door, paused on its threshold. "An' while yo're bein' so huffy with me, you might find out a few things—it might change yore mind some. . . . Eph Gowan's the one who steered this Jordan up here. What do yuh think of that?" he flung over his shoulder, and disappeared.

Old Cole, his visage mottled, was about to fling hot words after him, but at this last he caught himself.

There had been something about Kirk Jordan's forthright demeanor which had appealed to his grudging respect. But now that was washed away as completely as if it had never been.

"Gowan, eh?" he muttered, little ridges of muscle springing out along the line of his jaw. "We'll jest look into this."

9

"You'll make out all right?" Joan asked Kirk.

"Yes, don't worry about me."

Kirk swung up and headed out into the buffeting sand. To his relief, the storm seemed to be slacking off as he climbed higher. The dun fog lightened to grey, he could see a matter of yards around him. His breath came easier and even the bronc plucked up energy.

Before he reached the little spread in the Upper Basin he came into an area of comparative coolness, where almost no sand blew. Nor, it appeared, had the storm more than skirted this high ground. It was a load off his chest.

Pecos he found waiting with some anxiety.

"So yuh got back finally, huh?" said the little man. "I was beginnin' to wonder. Looks pretty stormy down below!"

Kirk grinned. "Regular Red Desert twister," he confessed. "It's sure kind of surprising to me it didn't get up this far, to speak of."

"Yeh—kind of a steady cool wind down off the mountain. That must hold it off."

The sky was coppery and opaque for the remainder of that day. Kirk was pleased that by the following morning the sun was out in its full glory. From the barrier ridge, the rim of the desert showed once more clearly.

"That's the end of that storm," Pecos grunted, as they ate breakfast. "Wonder how Cole Hutchinson looks at things today?" Kirk had told him of the fury of the storm which enveloped the Ladder outfit.

"If these storms continue," Kirk judged, "the same thing'll happen to him what happened to Eph Gowan—he'll find himself with a ranch on his hands and no grass!"

Pecos studied him, frowning. "Wonder how long it'll be before he decides to move into this basin?" he growled. "Ain't much question that's what he's savin' it fer."

Kirk passed it off then. Not long after, his partner found him saddling up. "Where to?" Pecos inquired. Kirk explained that he intended to ride to Beartrack Crossing for the mail. Presently he was jogging away from the J Bar and down the hills. His mien was cheerful and a song hovered on his lips.

Beartrack was a crossing on Havasu Creek, which threaded a deep and rocky canyon a score of miles to the north. There was Hazen's saloon, a small blacksmith shop and two or three abandoned, tumble-down buildings. The whole place had a weathered, sleepy appearance which belied its reputation. It was said to be tough, a gateway to back-mountain fastnesses where rustlers, horse thieves and the small fry of the lawless hid out.

Kirk reached the crossing without having met anyone on the trail.

Broke Hazen's place went under the name of a hotel. One side of the building housed the bar; the other was an "office." Behind a scarred and dented desk hung a rack where half-a-dozen outlying ranches were accustomed to look for their mail, which came through by stage once a week.

Down in front of the blacksmith shop stood a clump of hipshot broncs, and at the rack before Hazen's a single pony waited. Something quickened in Kirk as he recognized the animal. As he was getting down beside it, a trim figure emerged from Hazen's office-door. Kirk looked up into Joan Hutchinson's face.

His hat was off instantly. "This is a pleasant surprise," he drawled easily.

There was a faint twinkle in her steady eyes. "Is it?" She came down the steps, and for several moments they conversed with the freedom of old friends.

A shadow crossed the girl's face as she told of the inroads the sandstorm had made on the Ladder ranch. A number of steers had been found dead, and more grass was buried. "If it goes on, I don't know what Father will do."

Kirk helped her into the saddle. "Heading for home? I'll ride along a ways—" He swung up also.

Her smile broke through. "I thought you had come for your mail, Kirk!"

He flushed. He had forgotten it. But his wit was quick. "I daresay you looked, and can tell me whether there's anything in my box."

It was her turn to redden. "No, there isn't. That is—there was mail only in two other boxes, the Hanson's and the Kyle's."

Kirk chuckled. "That'll satisfy me."

They rode slowly down the canyon and along the hills. There seemed plenty to talk about, though her father or Buck Hutchinson were not mentioned. They found honest pleasure in each other's company, and it was only within a couple of miles of the Ladder ranch that Kirk took his leave and branched up the slopes toward the Upper Basin.

Nor was this their only meeting in that fashion. Each Friday Kirk dropped whatever he was busy with and saddling up, jogged blithely down the hills in the face of his persistent failure to bring back any mail.

It was not long before Pecos caught on. He narrowed his shrewd eyes and squinted calculatingly at Kirk. "If yuh don't mind my sayin' so," he remarked with something of an edge, "it's plumb dynamite to be buzzin' around that Hutchinson girl."

Kirk revealed no surprise, but his face froze up. "What gave you that idea?" he countered.

Pecos threw pretense aside. "I know because I know yuh! I ain't missed yore foggin' off every mail-day. But it ain't me yuh got to worry about. How 'bout them rumhounds down there at Beartrack, though? Yuh don't reckon it misses them—"

"What are you driving at?" Kirk rasped.

"Once word gets back to the Ladder outfit what's goin' on, you'll find out plenty fast!" Pecos threw back. "Or won't it bother yuh to walk into a mess of Ladder gun-throwers?"

Kirk stared. "Nonsense! There's no good getting spooky about this!"

Pecos was frankly defiant. "Go 'head the way you're goin', that's all! It'll be up to me to drag yuh out of a jackpot, if anybody can—an' I s'pose I'm jest fool 'nough to do it!"

Kirk shrugged. Saddling up and riding away from the cabin, Kirk came to certain conclusions.

Pecos was certainly right. And the only way Kirk knew to avert eventualities was to con- solidate his own strength, entrench his position, take Joan away from the Ladder ranch. A thrill ran through him at thought of asking her to marry him. Would she consent? It was a chance he must take. Yet he couldn't ask her to come here, to such a life.

That evening he said to Pecos: "I took a good look around, today. We've got something better here than graze for a hundred head of steers."

Pecos grunted, one bushy eye cocked.

"We've got to lay hands on some money," Kirk went on abruptly. "We'll put more steers on this range, hire a couple of extra hands. It's a waste of time to wait for the calf increase."

His grizzled partner followed his train of thought better than Kirk supposed. "Who can yuh touch fer enough?"

Kirk mused: "Well, there's Clem Chew. I've got his address, back East. I imagine hoeing a flower garden has about got him in shape now to consider investing in cows again."

Pecos said, "Well, yuh can try 'im."

Kirk spent a long time over the composition of the letter he meant to send to old Clem. It had to be put just right. When it was done he chafed until he was in the saddle and headed for Beartrack Crossing, where he would mail it.

Reaching the crossing, and pulling up before Hazen's, Kirk was surprised to find Joan's mount there before him. This was Thursday—the day before mail-day. She must have some letters to get off too. He slid out of the hull, reached the porch in three long strides, mounted and stepped inside.

There were several loungers in the office. The girl was talking to Broke Hazen at the desk. She turned as Kirk's boots rapped the floor, and to his amazement, swift apprehension sprang into her eyes.

Even as he touched his hat, smiling, the question shot through him—What did it mean? He dropped his letter in the post-box and stepped back; and in that moment he had his answer. Some instinct warned him to glance toward the door giving upon the bar. In it, lounging heavily, an air of immense power in his blocky body, stood Buck Hutchinson. His somber eyes raked Kirk's face.

"Jordan, I want a word with you!"

Kirk knew what was coming. The swooping tension which held this room was proof enough of what all expected. His tone was cool and brusque:

"I daresay you can have it—if you make it short."

Buck broke his immobility, swaggering through. He stopped a bare three strides from Kirk and swayed on his toes, settling his heels firmly.

"Have you been followin' my sister down here and monkeyin' around 'er?"

Kirk's face slowly darkened with wrath. He could find no words he would spend on this man.

"I *hear* you have!" Buck persisted gratingly. "Snatchin' our range first, an' then our women—you damn sneak!"

There was something impossible about the moment. The lightning of Kirk's eyes left Hutchinson a moment, flicking toward Joan. He was asking her a mute question; he was asking her to go while there was time.

Whether she misunderstood or not he never knew. She was gazing at Buck with an expression of outraged loathing, and turned impulsively to Kirk. Her words were tense:

"I am not his 'woman'! He is not even my brother!"

It was as though she disclaimed responsibility or interest in what was to happen. Yet Kirk was jarred. Not her brother? But how—

She interpreted his look. "Kirk, *watch him!* He means nothing to me—nothing!"

That was a blow to Buck. Its impact showed in the dull flush of his heavy, brutal features. It was true that he was no blood relation to Joan. Her father had married his mother, and he had been a man grown before he had ever laid eyes on her.

It more than half explained the antagonism which had always existed between Buck and Cole Hutchinson. The older man strongly suspected what was in Buck's mind, and wholly disapproved. Buck was in love with Joan. He meant to have her and have the Ladder ranch too. At first only a threat to the Ladder's extensive range, Buck now saw Kirk Jordan as a threat to his possession of the girl. It made him see red. He meant to wipe Kirk out.

Buck forgot his gun. No weapon could be of use to him now. He meant to use his hands, feel his enemy's bones crack and his neck snap. He came forward, crouching.

Suddenly he feinted, his beam-like arm curving in. The blow halted, and his other arm swung in, a steam-hammer stroke. Kirk swiftly side-stepped, laid a stinging blow alongside Buck's jaw, and was away again. Buck outweighed him by fifty pounds. He must count on that.

Suddenly Buck rushed. There was the ferocity of a bull in that charge. Kirk met it with chopping right and left swings, backing swiftly. Buck got in one heavy slug that rocked his head.

Then Kirk smashed into the desk. He could go no farther. Seeing that, Buck plunged. They came together with a thud, wrestled for a moment lying across the desktop, and crashed off to the floor.

Buck kicked and gouged in demoniac fury. Guarding desperately, Kirk jabbed at his face again and again, punishing blows that brought animal-like grunts to the heavier man's crushed lips.

Suddenly Kirk scrambled free of those huge arms and on to his feet. Buck lunged up, bored in like an insensate demon. His fist lashed out. Fire burst through Kirk's ribs; he thought one of them was broken. Weakness flooded him. Buck came on, poising another sledge-like blow.

Desperation swept Kirk forward. They were at each other in a fury of infighting. Chairs clattered out of their way; watching men hastily made for clear space. For Kirk the room seemed to grow dark and his breath shortened. A weight pressed on him.

In a moment of sudden opportunity he set himself, drew his arm back. Buck's massive head came up. Kirk let him have all he had, flush on the point of the jaw.

Buck abruptly straightened, his arms flinging outward. He stood a timeless moment while terrible surprise ran over his face. Then with a twist he smashed down.

Kirk's eye swept the room. He was looking for Buck's friends, wary of treachery. Men in the doors stared, wooden-faced, unmoving. Joan was pressed against the wall, her face blanched.

"I expect that settles it," he said thickly. He found himself looking at the girl. "Sorry—Joan. Had to—do it."

There was something new in her face, pale as she was. "It's all right, Kirk! I'm glad."

They had this moment of mutual understanding. Then Joan turned and passed out at the door, the men there opening to let her through. She went to her pony, swung up. Kirk followed her, oblivious of keen stares directed at his face.

Without words, Kirk and the girl slowly rode away along the canyon trail.

10

Cole Hutchinson sat in a rawhided chair on the gallery of the Ladder ranch house. Buck stood beside him, with no grace in his heavy, bull-like body. It was midmorning; the sun glared over the range, its heat pounding the brown soil in waves.

Cole's toughened, weather-beaten face was long. "I dunno what it's comin' to," he growled. "That last storm wiped out a thousand acres of as good range as we got—"

"You know the answer," Buck threw in. "I've been at yuh for months to pick up, lock, stock and barrel, and move up the slope! If we leave this Jordan in possession a few months longer," he added sullenly, "there won't be much excuse for the move when we finally come to it!"

Cole flared: "Suppose you let me manage that end of it! I got less faith in yore talk than I have in what yuh do!" His baleful glance rested momentarily on the still-unhealed breaks marring the other's broad face. "If yuh had to go fightin', yuh could at least have made sure of the outcome." He snorted. "Fer Gawd's sake, Buck!"

Buck flushed dully. His stepfather's words made him feel no easier in mind. He had the uncomfortable feeling that the entire range felt the same about his fight at Beartrack. With half-a-dozen witnesses there had been no opportunity to hush up his defeat at Kirk Jordan's hands.

Buck's hatred of Kirk for having whipped him was bitter. He only bided his time for a decisive retaliation. Meanwhile his hate reached out to include everyone who knew of his defeat. It was no task to include his stepfather in that circle. Buck had always felt a certain contempt for the older man. His name was not Hutchinson. It was Gandy. But he had been called Hutchinson so long, considered a Hutchinson man, one of the family, that at times he felt Cole's iron conservatism a drag on him he would do anything to throw off.

Times without number he would have ridden away from the Ladder spread, not to return. But there was Joan. He knew the effect his whipping must have on the girl's opinion of him. It made him frantic, reckless. He wanted to bushwhack Kirk, except that he knew such a course would turn Joan against him forever.

He had seen an out in the hope of driving Kirk and his partner out of the Upper Basin. And now old Cole held off for some stubborn, hidebound reason he refused to so much as explain.

There would have been a hot argument there on the ranch gallery, had it not been for the horseman who pounded in across the yard and drew up in a swirl of dust. There was a portent in the man's face which drew Cole half out of his chair.

"What is it, Decker?" he barked.

The puncher flashed: "I jest run across a slew of down steers—eight or ten of 'em, Cole! Every last one of 'em drilled between the eyes!"

Cole was on his feet, now; commanding despite his age. A thunderous scowl sat on his brows.

Watching him narrowly, Buck was galvanized with hope by what he saw. "Jordan's work!" he hurled out ungovernably. "By God, that's goin' too far! I'll take care of this!"

Before he could turn away, Cole threw out a hand. "Hold on, hyar! Yuh won't do nothin' of the kind, Buck! I'll see to it!"

Buck stared at him incredulously. Cole meant to ride up the hills, of course. That he might go alone was unheard-of. Someone must go along with him, to back his move. Buck meant to be there. He could depend on his ability to wrest matters out of the older man's hands at the crucial time.

"I'll get some of the boys!" he said swiftly.

"Come back hyar!" Cole bellowed. His eyes flamed with an authority that was not old. "You'll stay right where you are!" he pointed out sternly. "The time ain't come yet when I can't give orders on this ranch, an' make 'em stick!"

He speared Buck with a glare. The latter subsided, fuming. Let the old fool have his way,

Buck was thinking. There's plenty of time.

Cole whirled on the puncher. "Saddle a bronc fer me," he snapped. As the man left, he strode into the house and emerged buckling on a cartridge-belt and worn-handled Colt which he had not worn for months.

Buck angrily watched him walk across the ranch yard. Decker met him with a restless bronc. Cole mastered it with iron hand. He swung up, turned his mount's head toward the rising slopes and jogged away.

Heavy were the thoughts which boiled through Cole's mind as he rode upward. He had no slightest doubt that Kirk Jordan had been responsible for the slain steers. For a fleeting moment, pensive regret assailed him. He recalled Kirk vividly, though they had met only once, some time ago now. There had been good mettle in that fellow. Steered straight, he would have gone far.

But there had been only one attitude to take against Jordan, of course. Seeing what he was, and was doing, he couldn't be allowed any kind of interest in Joan. Yet it might be because of the very words which had passed in the Ladder house, that day of the storm, that Jordan had taken this means of retaliation.

Cole's jaw corded. "He went too far!" he growled. "There won't be no doubt of that left in his mind when I get done with him!"

He knew the Upper Basin thoroughly, though

he had not been near it in five years. Brad Rock had told him where Jordan had built his cabin. Cole circled to come on the place unwarningly; not because he feared he might not otherwise reach it, but because he didn't want to be seen too soon. No use giving Jordan too much time to think up what he would say.

He reached the pine-clad ridge in which the J Bar gate had been built, and turned along it. At one point the ridge approached within a quarter-mile of the new cabin standing in the open, beside Feather Creek. Cole kept to the trees, his jaws set with his dour thinking; but when at last he turned straight toward the cabin, it was he who suffered a surprise.

Without any warning, a mounted Indian appeared squarely in his trail, a rifle across his knees.

Cole jerked his bronc back, startled. Slumbering wrath burst forth sharply. His hand gripped his six-gun convulsively and half-drew the weapon.

The Apache's shot whipped past his bronc's head, missing only by inches. The pony whirled, snorting—plunged into the protecting pines at a tangent.

"So Jordan's got Injuns doin' his dirty work now!" the rancher whipped out fiercely. "We'll see 'bout this!" He jammed in the spurs and set a curving course which should bring him out into the open half-a-mile away. From there he would strike toward the cabin on the flat. He had to gamble on Kirk's being there. Once a witness to this stalking, he'd have to call off his red devils.

Cole's mount flashed through the pines on a dead run. His gun was out now—no taking chances with this set-up! He felt he was getting away, when suddenly a carbine crashed on his right; an unearthly screech rent the sun-drenched quiet.

He muffled a curse, flinging a shot into the scrub by way of warning. At this rate, he'd never reach the open at all. It was no good expecting to count on Jordan's intercession unless he succeeded.

In quick succession then, two more gunshots rang out immediately to the fore. The ridge was simply bristling with savages! To his dismay he found himself crowded steadily leftward, away from the J Bar and toward, in all probability, a sordid fate in the center of desolation at the hands of these ruthless devils.

Crash! The short, vicious burst of an Indian carbine broke out behind him now, at no great distance. He felt a tug at his hat. No doubt about their determination to finish him!

Spat! There was that nagging fire from the fore. Cole was astounded at how little of themselves the foe showed him. He had not got in one good shot yet.

The last slug, snarling off his tapadero, made

95

up his mind. He wheeled toward a jumble of rocks on the only side open to him and plunged desperately toward them. If he could only get that far and hole up—

"This way!" a call reached him. He flung a look. Kirk Jordan sat a lathered bronc on the crest of a little rise not far from the rocks. Cole gulped. He hadn't known how deep a hole he'd got himself into; how badly he needed this help, till now!

He turned his pony toward the other man. He was there in a moment. Kirk only glanced at him to make sure of his whereabouts. Then he was facing the ring of pines.

A dozen Apaches, riding bareback like whirlwinds, swirled into the open. They meant to close in on Cole Hutchinson, yells ringing. They hauled in at sight of Kirk.

"Stop!" Kirk rifled. "This man is mine! I want him!"

One of the Indians pressed forward. He glared at Cole, then faced Kirk with inscrutable features. It was Straight Tongue.

"Him bad man," he argued shortly. "Him Hutch'son. Apache want him too!"

"I know who he is!" Kirk was stern. "And I know what to do with him! . . . What you are thinking is just, Straight Tongue. But I ask you to forego it this time."

The Indian thought it over. He looked back at

96

his grim-visaged fellows, and back at Cole. His decision was deliberate. Finally he nodded.

"We give him you, dis time," he muttered. " 'Nother time—" He broke off expressively.

Kirk watched Straight Tongue and the others turn and jog away. Not until they were gone from sight did he turn back to the rancher.

Cole's eyes were hard and diamond-bright.

"So I'm yore man, eh?" he queried challengingly.

"Shore," put in a new voice, coolly insolent. Pecos moved into sight and came forward. "If it wa'n't fer him, Hutchinson, jest where'd yuh be about now?"

Cole eyed them both severely. He was not taken aback. He had come here to talk about one thing.

"Jordan, I've had to thank yuh before, and I'm doin' it again. But it don't change anything. Maybe you'll explain to me why you shot a bunch of my steers—or had it done!"

Pecos burst out harshly: "Why, dang yore ornery hide—" But Kirk only measured Cole quietly with his eyes. His words were deadly calm.

"I had nothing to do with any steer-shooting, Hutchinson. If any happened, this is the first I've heard of it."

Cole's tone had the flick of a whip. "How 'bout hirin' redskins to do yore dirty work for yuh?"

"I've done no hiring," Kirk retorted patiently.

"Your son started this business when he hung that Apache a while back, up on Geronimo Mountain."

This should have surprised Cole, but it did not. He had heard of the occurrence, if not from Buck. He took refuge in an oblique attack.

"Yuh was mighty handy today, when it come to stallin' the sneakin' devils off!" he declared pointedly.

Kirk's features flushed. Only the fact that this man was Joan's father made his words moderate. "Where I happened to be has got nothing to do with it. You should be thankful I was in earshot when the first shots went off!"

"Wal—" Cole retracted skilfully. "Lookin' at it in that light, I reckon yo're right, Jordan." He pondered heavily. "Will yuh swear to me yuh had nothin' to do with shootin' down my steers?"

"Not again," Kirk told him sharply.

It was the right answer. Cole nodded approvingly. "Yuh did say so once," he conceded. "But Jordan, let me get this straight: Did Eph Gowan send yuh up here to ranch?" A curious hardness and implacability crept into his face. "Is Gowan coverin' yuh with these Apache devils?"

Kirk's tone was wooden. "No man sends me anywhere."

"What yuh aimin' to do with me?"

The answer was stony silence. In that moment Cole realized that Kirk's had been the only method by which he could have taken any man from the vengeful Apaches. They had been bent on his death. Only Kirk's pressing what they could have considered a prior claim would have had the slightest weight with them. It revealed, at the same time, the extent of their faith in Kirk.

"Wal—" Cole's voice was muffled. "Kinda looks like I spoke outa turn a time or two. . . . But don't get the idea I'm backin' away from yuh, Jordan! Yo're on my range! You've made trouble enough fer half-a-dozen men! Take a well-meant warnin' an' pull out."

Pecos spoke up at last, dryly. "How 'bout takin' yore own advice?"

The veins stood out on Cole's bony forehead and his leathery cheeks snapped lean. He glared at Pecos fiercely for a taut moment. Then suddenly he surprised them with a tight grin.

"Reckon that's puttin' it plain 'nough," he nodded. Without more ado, he swung his bronc and started to jog down the slope of the basin the way he had come.

But he was thoughtful as he rode, and all was not well with him. "Kinda looks like them hombres stumped me!" he grunted.

11

Buck Hutchinson fumed about the Ladder ranch yard and corrals all the while Cole was gone, in a lather of foiled rage.

He had not given Joan more than a furtive glance and a few muffled words since she had witnessed his defeat at Kirk Jordan's hands, and he kept away from the house today. So it was that, staying in the open, he caught sight of Cole on his return.

He started forward to intercept Cole. The latter had got down in front of the bunkhouse, to turn his bronc over to one of the punchers lounging there. Buck came barging around the back of the log building, and was on the point of charging into the open, dark of face and with recriminations on his tongue, when a few words arrested him. Just around the corner of the bunkhouse, where he could not be seen, he halted abruptly.

"Boss, whyn't yuh take a handful of us up there with yuh?" Len Decker was demanding of Cole.

"No." Cole's negative rolled out as firmly as ever. "If you hellions had been there when them danged redskins jumped me, there'd been blood spilled shore! It was jest the breaks of the game to have Jordan save my hide that-a-way. For the time bein' I ain't got no course but to swaller it."

"But hell, boss! If we go on losin' steers shot—"

"Jordan didn't have nothin' to do with that," Cole broke in.

"How do yuh know he didn't?"

"Because he swore he didn't; an' I believe him."

Standing hidden, Buck sneered. So Cole was taking Jordan's word for things, was he? Buck's scorn for such simplicity was unutterable.

"Wal, hang it all, I don't like it," broke in the voice of another of the punchers. "Jest tip us the word, boss, an' the whole crew'll fog up there. We'll lay off the nice stuff—clean Jordan an' his ten-cent outfit outa there quicker'n yuh could say Jack Robinson! Then yuh won't have to take his word fer anythin'!"

Cole's tone hardened to severity.

"You've been listenin' to Buck, ain't yuh? That's his kind of talk yo're givin' me now. . . . If yuh think this range fight is somethin' to settle off-hand that way, yo're all wrong."

"What yuh aimin' to do, then?"

Cole's measured tone revealed thought: "If we can freeze an' discourage Jordan out, same as we done to Eph Gowan, I reckon that'd be the best way."

The talk went on. Teeth gritted, Buck heard all that had taken place up there in the high basin.

Something steeled in him at thought of Kirk Jordan's easy victory over Cole. Then when he realized the significance of the note on which Kirk and Cole had parted, an idea flashed into his mind; an idea on which he proposed to act at once.

He wheeled away quickly. Making sure that he was not seen, he worked his way to a saddle shed. On the ground there, below the worn hulls hung on pegs, lay a jumbled pile of Ladder branding irons. With as little ado as possible, he selected a running iron suited to his purpose and thrust it inside the belt of his chaps. Then he turned back toward the corrals.

A few minutes later he was in the saddle and jogging away from the spread.

Steady climbing took him up the high slopes. He followed the pines for the most part, but paused occasionally to make sure he did not get beyond the natural grazing area of the Ladder stock. Within a mile or two of the Upper Basin, he was still able to spot a few straying Ladder steers.

Nodding his satisfaction with the circumstance, he fell to searching for calves. One he found, a brindled, cavorting little fellow; but it failed to suit him. He searched further. Finally he located two.

Both were for the moment separated from their mothers. Both had been ear-marked with the

Ladder notch, but neither was branded as yet. Buck unlimbered his rope, knocked the calves down and snared them with hogging-strings. Then he gathered twigs, built a fire, and branded the calves with a careful J Bar.

Finished, he released the calves and watched them hightail bawling into the deep brush. A hard smile, with no humor in it, twisted his leathery lips.

"Reckon that'll help things along," he muttered to himself. "A few more like that, an' maybe Cole won't be so anxious to swallow this Jordan hombre's every last word!"

In a couple of hours' time Buck concluded that enough Ladder calves were wearing the newly burned J Bar mark. He must be careful not to overdo it.

It was a day later that Kirk rode down through the pines above the J Bar from a long morning's work. He had discovered a clear, running spring in a wooded hollow some miles to the west, which would do wonderfully for a line camp when they began to expand, and was bent on telling Pecos about it.

To his irritation, at least momentarily, Pecos was nowhere in evidence about the little spread.

Kirk let out a shrill cowboy "Yipee-e!" and waited, but received no answer. It struck him that his partner might be somewhere out in the basin, and he rode toward the ridge. Climbing up through scrub growth to the pines, he at length emerged on a rocky ledge from which he could see far.

Nothing was in sight anywhere that gave a clue to the whereabouts of Pecos.

Kirk frowned. They had long since decided that it would not do to leave the ranch utterly deserted at any time, yet Pecos had done so now. It was not like him at all. It occurred to Kirk that Pecos might have met with an accident.

A band tightening around Kirk's chest, he pulled his bronc about and struck back toward the ranch yard. It was just possible that he could pick up sign in the dust there that would give a hint as to what direction Pecos had gone.

Reaching the level range, he came pelting through the brush and flashed around the corner of the cabin. He hauled up then, yanking his pony back on its haunches. Pecos was not there, but somebody else was. Two men on whom he had never before laid eyes were sitting their saddles before the cabin door.

They shot sharp looks across at him. There was a habitual wariness about them both which, at least, was familiar. Kirk did not need the glint of the star on that vest of the biggest of the pair to identify them.

His voice went thin with reserve.

"What do you two want?"

His sudden appearance had plainly surprised them. The hawk-faced sheriff eased himself in his saddle, in no hurry to speak up. He cleared his throat and countered.

"Who are yuh?"

"Kirk Jordan's my name. I run this spread."

The lawman's beady scrutiny never left his face.

"Wal, yo're bold 'nough about admittin' it!" And after a moment: "Where's yore pardner?"

"I'm asking you again," he pointed out. "Just what is it you want here?"

"Wal, I want you, fer one thing," the sheriff told him curtly. "—Jest leave yore hands crossed on the saddle horn, like yuh got 'em. Curly, ride up beside him an' relieve him of that belt gun an' his rifle."

"Jest a minute now!" Curley was saying, as he might soothe a fractious horse. "While I unloosen this here belt-catch. . . . All right, that's better!"

He swung Kirk's cartridge-belt deftly away, drawing the latter's rifle from its boot at the same time.

"This is mighty unfriendly work, Sheriff," Kirk said levelly. "A man can only put one meaning to it. Suppose you tell me what's behind it!"

The lawman's eyes flickered. "The charge is rustlin'," he replied dryly. "Not that I reckon yuh need to be told."

"Rustling! Why I—" Kirk broke off, hardening.

"Where did you get any such idea as that?"

The other was not interested in his reactions. "Where does a man usually git it?" he flung back, stingingly.

"The accusation doesn't come from Hutchinson, by any chance?"

"Wal, since it's Ladder calves that've been branded with yore iron," the sheriff rejoined, sarcastically, "I don't reckon there's anything queer 'bout it if it did come from there!"

"Calves?" Kirk caught him up sharply.

"Half-a-dozen of 'em," was the ready answer. "But not even botherin' to change Hutch's earmark was a mistake!"

"It was a mistake for somebody!" Kirk flashed. "And it'll be one for you, Sheriff, if you think I'd be such a fool! Brand Cole Hutchinson's calves? Why, a child would know better! His stock is brindle; mine mostly all black and white—"

He broke off, sensing the uselessness of argument, at the smile on the lawman's hatchet face.

"There shore ain't much sense to any o' this," the latter conceded. "But rustlers ain't notorious fer showin' sense, that I know of. . . . We'll jest take yuh along an' let yuh explain to the judge."

"You're not taking me anywhere! How do I know you're what you claim you are? Anybody can stick a badge on his vest and put up a bluff.

Right here and now is the first I ever heard of any rustling—yet you propose to pack me off to the cooler without so much as supporting your charge. . . . Nothing doing!"

The lawman showed signs of choler. He caught himself, however, his dry humor returning.

"Wal, if yuh don't reckon I'm a shore-'nough badge toter, mebby the judge can convince yuh of that too!" He dragged a pair of manacles out of his pocket. "Stick out yore paws!"

Kirk was desperate. He felt that once he allowed those steel cuffs to be snapped over his wrists he was helpless.

Kirk kicked his bronc in the flank, on the off side. The pony reared.

Cursing under his breath, the sheriff pushed forward. With a hard hand he jerked downward on Kirk's bridle.

"None o' yore tricks!" he ground out. "By Gawd, I'll stick these irons on yuh or know the reason why!"

"You'll never do it!" Kirk jerked out.

"So you say!"

Curly, the deputy, was bringing his six-gun up. His face was set and determined. Before he could complete his intention, a shot rang out near at hand and the gun sprang out of his fingers as though snatched.

Surprise gripped them all. The sheriff and his deputy whirled, their visages darkening. Behind them, at the corner of the cabin, Pecos Johnson leveled his stern gaze over the barrel of a gun.

"Jest stay like yuh are, gents," he intoned grimly.

12

Silence fell, thick and pregnant. The lawman stared at Pecos, his jaw dropped. Then it snapped shut.

"Yo're Jordan's pardner, ain't yuh" he rasped.

Coming forward, Pecos surveyed him coolly. "It happens I am—if it's any of yore damned business!" he grunted.

Kirk slid out of the saddle, and with two long strides reached Curly's side. He snatched his weapons up, clasped his cartridge-belt around his waist again.

"Wal, Kirk," Pecos drawled, "there's times when I'm reminded I don't know as much 'bout yore past life as I thought I did. What's all this about?"

There was no flippancy in Kirk's reply.

"This hombre is carrying a charge of rustling, brought against us by Hutchinson!"

"Ahuh." Pecos's faded eyes narrowed. "Reckon that explains a lot."

He looked shrewdly at the lawman. "Who are yuh?" he drew out, then, sharply.

"I'm Gabe Farrow, of Laguna." A dull red flush overspread Farrow's visage. "I'm doin' my duty—an' that's to break up rustlin' wherever I find it!"

"You're pretty sure you found some here, eh?" Kirk flung at him.

"Wal—I had it pointed out to me. Same thing. An' Johnson, yuh better put up that hog leg while yuh got a chance. I'll overlook yore shootin' Curly's gun out of his hand—"

Pecos laughed gruffly.

"Yuh will, huh? Reckon that's broad minded of yuh. Looks like it's up to us to overlook yore callin' us rustlers, if yuh turn tail an' ride back out of here without no more funny work. But don't run away with the idea that we're gentle!"

Farrow gnawed his stringy mustache. He became argumentative.

"I'm warnin' yuh it'll go hard with yuh if yuh keep up this bluff! If yuh swear yuh ain't been brandin' no Ladder calves, give up yore arms; ride in to town with me an' prove yore innocence," he advised, keeping ire out of his tone with an effort.

Pecos caught him up.

"Prove our innocence! Reckon that's 'bout the size of it, in this neck of woods. In the man's country I come from, a man's considered innocent till he's proven guilty!"

The lawman's flush grew hectic.

"Yo're jest bandyin' words now!"

"Isn't that what you've been doing since you showed up here?" Kirk threw in, thinly. "You know the set-up here. This is free range. My partner and I drove in a small herd and started to carve out a ranch for ourselves. The Ladder outfit says no. We've had all we could do to hold our own. Good Lord, man! Do you think we'd deliberately ask for trouble by branding Ladder stock on the side?"

"It's the way little outfits 've growed since I was knee-high to a grasshopper," Farrow retorted. "What makes you so different?"

"You're going at this all wrong, Sheriff," Kirk declared. "Letting Hutchinson make a cat's paw of you may mean enough votes to make it worthwhile, but—"

"Oh hell, Kirk!" Pecos interjected, roughly. "Give 'im his walkin' papers an' toss him off the ranch!"

Farrow whirled on Pecos, his bony cheeks whitening with anger.

"Yo're in a position to do that, Johnson. But I wouldn't advise yuh to, unless yo're ready to pick up and leave this range overnight. For if I go away from here empty handed today, I'll be back, an' I'll bring a posse big 'nough to settle this deal one way or 'nother an' no mistake!"

"The whole Ladder outfit, I reckon?" Pecos snapped.

"Hold on, Pecos," Kirk took charge. "Sheriff, you're mighty free with your accusations, and it's got me curious. Have you got evidence to back it up—or did you take Hutchinson's word for it?"

"Shore, I've got evidence!" Farrow was belligerent. "Four or five calves, brindles, with the Ladder ear-notch an' brand-new J Bar brands!"

"Who showed 'em to yuh—Buck Hutchinson?" Pecos queried, thinly.

A vein throbbed in the lawman's forehead. "Damn yuh, Johnson, why shouldn't he show 'em to me?" he roared.

Pecos would have discharged a fiery response, but Kirk waved him to silence.

"Where did you see these calves, Farrow?"

"Down the slope here, not three miles from yore cabin!"

His tone convinced Kirk that he was speaking the truth. It seemed to preclude any chance of proving that this charge was a trumped-up affair.

"Could you find them again?"

Farrow's snort was scornful. "If I didn't think my chances was purty good, would I be fool 'nough to come here with the intention of ridin' the two of yuh down to court?"

Kirk thought a moment, his lips thin.

"We'll all ride down there and take a look," he decided.

"Kirk, have yuh lost yore mind?" Pecos blurted.

Kirk's smile was tight.

"Not so's you could notice it," was the reply. "I want to find out for myself what kind of a job they're ringing in on us!"

Pecos grumbled, but he crawled into his saddle.

He had put up his gun, but he kept a wary watch of the lawmen, and made a gesture indicating that they were to ride ahead.

"I want yuh where I can keep an eye on yuh!"

Kirk rode beside Farrow as they headed toward the basin's rim, in the direction of the desert.

The sheriff rode across several pine ridges, threaded small grassy meadows, and then began to pay particular attention to landmarks. He came to a little hollow, looked around swiftly, and led on. There were no calves in sight, and no Ladder steers either, though this was Ladder range.

Farrow seemed plainly at fault now. He began to loop backward and up, his keen eyes sweeping. His leathery lips drew into a thin line. Finally he drew in. Kirk looked at him, wondering what was in the man's mind.

"Well, Farrow. We're waiting to see those calves!"

Suddenly the lawman whirled, his visage scarlet, and leveled a quivering, accusative finger at Pecos.

"Damn yuh, yuh rode along behind me an' hazed them calves away into the brush where they couldn't be found, Johnson!" he roared.

Pecos scrutinized him with significant calm.

"What yuh drivin' at now?" he retorted. "Can't find yore evidence—is that it?"

"Yuh know that's it; an' yuh know why, too!"

113

Farrow bellowed, beside himself with chagrin. "I tell yuh—"

"Hold that!" Pecos's words crackled like static in the dry air. "Farrow, I didn't even know yuh existed, much less what yuh was up to, till I rode in on yuh there at the ranch! Seein' yore pardner get gay with a gun was 'nough to make me horn in first an' find out what it was all about afterwards."

Farrow stared at him with the rage of defeat in his beady pupils.

"Somethin' mighty damn queer is bein' pulled off here!" he burst out. "Them branded calves was here, an' I seen 'em, not three hours ago! Now they're gone! What's the answer?"

Pecos grunted.

"Reckon it's up to you to supply that. But I'd think twice 'bout bringin' charges of rustlin' another time, if yuh ain't got no better grounds to base it on than yuh got now!"

Farrow was fuming, stung and sore as a hurt bear. Even Curly was staring around, slack jawed, as if he couldn't understand what had happened.

"Wal, Kirk," said Pecos, "we might's well ride back up to the ranch. We got somethin' to do, whether these fellers have or not!"

But Kirk did not turn away immediately.

"Where did you see those calves, Farrow?" he queried. "We'll have a look and see what the sign says."

114

"They was over there—" the lawman responded, pointing.

They rode over, even Pecos reluctantly following. To the manifest surprise of the sheriff and his deputy, no cattle tracks showed there or anywhere near, save very old ones.

Farrow scratched his head. "Damn if I savvy it!" he growled. "Must've been in 'nother hollow we seen 'em—an' yet, this *must* be the one!" He was wholly bewildered.

"Well—" Kirk was terse. "I don't know why I should help you hunt up evidence for a charge of rustling against myself, Farrow. You ran your bluff, and you couldn't make it stick." His tone roughened. "Consider yourself warned what'll happen to you the next time you show up on the J Bar with any such cock-and-bull story as this one!"

Farrow sputtered, his face red and white by turns. His hands were nervous. They strayed toward his six-gun and away again. He knew only too well that some trick was being played on him, and he failed to grasp what it was. His wrath seethed.

"Reckon I ain't got no choice but to let yuh go, Jordan," he choked. "But you can keep yore threats to yoreself. Yuh bet I'll be showin' up again the minute I git the straight o' this!"

"It wants to be damned straight, then!" Pecos threw in, coldly. "An' if yo're figgerin' to come at me the same way again, yuh better come a'smokin'!"

With that they parted, Kirk and Pecos turning back up the slopes. Neither spoke until they were beyond earshot of the lawmen. Then the gnarled little man shot an inquiring glance at his companion.

"What yuh make of it, Kirk?"

"Hanged if I know!"

"Yuh figgerin' Farrow never laid eyes on them branded calves at all?"

"No—he saw them all right. It seems pretty plain that Hutchinson would make sure of that."

"Then what—" Pecos broke off, his jaw dropping. "Well, I'll be damned!" he ejaculated, forcibly. "Reckon it never struck me till jest this minute!"

"What?"

"Why—them danged Apaches of Gowan's! That's the answer, Kirk, shore as shootin'!"

Kirk nodded. "I thought of that, myself. There doesn't seem to be any other answer, and that's a fact."

"Why, shore!" Pecos broke in, quickly. "I thought I was doin' pretty well by bein' away when Farrow showed up, so's I could get the bulge on him before he got the irons clapped onto yuh. But them redskins—reckon they seen through it all from the beginnin'. Nobody but them would know how to spirit them calves away, wipe out their sign slick as a whistle, an' leave old tracks untouched." There was a hint of marvelling in his tone. "Danged if I ain't gettin' a better opinion of 'em as time goes on! . . . Kirk, what'll yuh do 'bout Hutchinson?"

Kirk was silent for a long time.

"Nothing," he decided finally.

13

Pecos saw something in Kirk's manner that was unusual the moment the latter rode up to the ranch. Kirk had ridden down to Beartrack for the mail.

"What's up?" Pecos queried, shrewdly.

Kirk slid out of the hull and came toward him, producing an envelope as he did so.

"Letter from old Clem—"

"Huh! He turn yuh down?"

"Not much!" Suddenly Kirk grinned happily. "He sent me a draft on Santa Fe. I'll have to ride out and cash it."

"Big 'nough to be worthwhile?"

"Enough to put another hundred head of steers here in the basin, if I spread it."

Pecos was more pleased than he showed. "Wal—better get ready an' rare into it," was his comment.

"I'm going to. I don't intend to lose no time."

Since the ride to Santa Fe was a long one, Kirk decided to start at once. His best clothes came out of his war-bag and for a time he was busy slicking up. Pecos surveyed these preparations wooden-faced.

"Feller'd think yuh was gettin' married, stead of goin' to pick up a bunch of cows."

Kirk's grin flashed out again. "Can't tell what's

liable to come up," he responded banteringly.

He was away half-an-hour later on a fresh bronc. He made a score of miles before darkness overtook him, and camped in the open. Over his small fire he had time for thought, and Joan Hutchinson returned to his mind.

"Queer I didn't see her at the Crossing," he mused. He would have given much to have shared his good-news with her. "But maybe she's gone on a trip somewhere." He knew from her talk that she often did take such trips.

Late afternoon of the next day saw Kirk jogging across the broad sweep of sagebrush which led up to Santa Fe on its bench. An hour later he rode into the plaza.

Slouching *mestizos*, blanketed Indians, army men crowded the walks. Huge freights piled high with buffalo hides from the Panhandle rumbled by. Shaggy ponies filled the tie-racks. A guitar tinkled. Kirk glanced up at the American flag atop the military post, noted the blue uniformed sentries below, and smiled. Although he had not been thinking about it when Clem Chew's letter arrived, he was glad to walk once more in this busy mart of men.

He put up his bronc in a wagon-yard and strolled out to a hash house and ate. He was wondering how he was to spend his evening, when a figure on the street before him arrested his gaze.

"Is that—it can't be—" he murmured his amazement.

He hurried, caught up; and found himself looking down into Joan Hutchinson's face.

Her surprise was as great as his. "Why, Kirk! How in the world did you get here?"

He wanted to tell her his good fortune in a rush of words; then the desire to have his great news a little longer proved stronger. He told her business had brought him, and kept the talk on herself. She was staying with Major Kernan and his wife, she said: old friends of her father's.

"What are you doing tonight?" he pursued.

Her face slightly fell, then brightened again. "Kirk, there is going to be a dance at the fort tonight, and I have promised to go. . . . But there's no reason why you can't come too—"

"Well—" Kirk was both anxious and dubious.

At that moment, Major Kernan himself appeared, with several fellow officers. Seeing Joan, he detached himself and came forward, his campaign hat sweeping off gracefully. He was a lank, capable-looking, sandy-haired man of forty-five. Southwestern suns had refined his strict features to an appearance of keen intelligence.

Joan introduced him to Kirk. Kernan saw at once in what quarter the wind lay. A smile hovered beneath his jaunty military mustache.

"Why not take in the hop tonight, Jordan?"

Kirk demurred: "I don't know if I—"

"Nonsense. You may consider this an invitation. Glad to accommodate one of Joan's friends— hope we'll be friends too."

Kirk's difficulties melted. He was so pleased that it did not bother him that the major should carry Joan off to Officer's Row for dinner on the spot.

Yet he chafed at the slow passage of time. The dance was to begin at ten. For an hour he prowled the plaza, bought himself a new silk kerchief, and half-smoked cigarettes. It was slightly after ten o'clock when he presented himself at the fort.

The dance had already begun. The military band was in fine fettle, the bold strains of a waltz flowing out into the velvet night.

The building was a converted barracks. But it had been transformed with draperies of bunting, swinging lamps, and masses of decorative evergreen from Taos Mountain.

Kirk joined the stag line on his arrival. Some young lieutenant was dancing with Joan when he first spied her. But at the end of the dance, Kirk cut in, claimed the girl. She was willing enough; even the scowling lieutenant noticed it.

But after the first two dances, Kirk's path was far from smooth. Joan, in a high-waisted gown and old-gold earrings which set her off delightfully, was a lodestone to every young blood in the hall. They vied with one another in ingenious ruses to deprive Kirk of her company.

121

The girl took it in better part than he, but she was willing enough, after a siege of several hectic dances, to agree on his suggestion that they slip away for a time.

They left the gaiety and bright lights; found themselves in the soft shadows of trees fringing the parade ground. The moon had risen. It cast an effulgence of silver over the world which exerted a spell of its own.

"No evening could be more perfect," Joan murmured.

Kirk saw that now was the moment for his great news. With a controlled, low-toned voice he told her of his plan to enlarge his J Bar spread—of his writing for a loan, and receiving it; and the great plans this opened for the future.

"We'll build a ranch equal to the Ladder," he declared. "How does that strike you, Joan?"

"Oh, Kirk!" She was glad for him. It showed more in her manner than in her words.

Kirk sensed something of her feelings. He sobered.

"I'm afraid this will only set your father against me harder than ever," he said slowly.

They looked into each other's eyes. The moonlight bathed Joan's gentle features in a beauty Kirk had never beheld. Something welled in him. It showed in his own dark eyes.

"Joan—"

Suddenly they were in each other's arms. It had been as spontaneous as an explosion.

"Joan, will you marry me?"

"Of course, darling!"

He was still insistent. "At once?"

She sighed. "If you like."

He caught her pensiveness. "Of course if you'd rather not—"

Her arms tightened, her chuckle was indulgent. "Silly, it's just that I'm—a girl. We like to dream about these things, I suppose; hug them to us for a time. But this will be so sudden."

He was relieved.

"We'll get married tomorrow. Joan, I can hardly wait! . . . But there's much to do."

"Yes," she said thoughtfully. "Much indeed." She was thinking of her father again. She knew what this would mean to Cole. It would be a blow, and a terrible one. She could only hope it would not seem to him deliberate. She turned to Kirk impulsively: "Darling, when Father learns—"

His understanding was quick. "Joan, I know how you feel. Let me be the one to tell him. I'll do it as sensibly and quietly as possible."

She looked at him with eyes of love. "I know you will. If it weren't for that—"

There was much to talk of. The rest of the evening passed like a dream for Kirk.

Kirk saw her to the Kernan home a couple of hours before dawn. When their announcement was made to the Major and Mrs. Kernan, the latter insisted Kirk remain for a betrothal breakfast; but Kirk was adamant in his refusal. There was too much to do.

He left in a sweat of impatience for the banks to open. But with a marriage to go through, a herd of steers to purchase and drive across the desert, he didn't lack for something to do. Before the bank finally threw open its doors at nine o'clock, Kirk had already engaged two punchers to help him drive his cattle west as soon as he procured it.

He went to the bank then, cashed his draft, and returned to the Kernans'. Joan was waiting for him, flushed and pretty. In two hours' time they were married by the army chaplain, the Major and his wife witnessing.

A gay wedding breakfast followed; and then, almost at once, the pain of parting.

"I'll remain here for three days, dear," Joan told him, her warm arms encircling his neck. "Then I'll start home. That should give you time to do what you have to. . . . And may the days fly!"

He laughed gruffly. "But not too fast. I'll be working like mad, sweet. I must find the stock I want, make my dicker, and then drive it."

They wrenched apart at last. There was something a little unreal for Kirk about the whole thing. Married! It was incredible. Incredible not only that he should have done it, but that Joan had consented. What would Pecos have to say?

With his two punchers, he rode south down the valley of the Rio Grande. Vast cattle ranches spread out, farms, Indian pueblos. Kirk searched diligently for precisely the stock he wanted, but it was the second day before he found it. Then it was a matter of long argument as to price. Slowly the price came down within his reach. Still unsatisfied, he pretended to ride away. The rancher let him go, then rode after him. They made a deal in a few minutes, and Kirk was the owner of six score head of prime beef steers.

They got them cut out that day, by dint of herculean labor. Kirk insisted on starting them west. In the morning, after an impatient night, the little herd streamed away into the desert.

It was the next day that their slow progress brought them to the Chimayo stage-station, fifty miles west of Santa Fe. Kirk rode in as a matter of course.

The agent met him at the door. "Better hold that herd here a few days, if yuh think anythin' of it," he told Kirk.

"How's that?"

"Apaches on a rampage," was the answer. "I hear there's half-a-hundred or so on the tear—wiped out two-three little ranches over in the Blue Mountains."

Kirk's gaze narrowed. The Blues were no great

distance from Geronimo Mountain. He said sharply: "Stage go through?"

"Yeh—"

"Any women on it?"

The agent nodded. "Old Hutchinson's girl went through."

Something tightened Kirk's chest as he turned away. "Thanks," he said shortly. "Reckon I'll push on."

14

Gabe Farrow, of Laguna, was far from satisfied with the results of his attempt to lay the proof of his own guilt before Kirk Jordan. He let Jordan and Pecos Johnson go because he had to, but he did not allow the matter to drop there.

For several days he and his deputy remained in the neighborhood of Geronimo Mountain. They combed the brush painstakingly for miles around the spot where the calves had been last seen. The fact that his search was fruitless did not discourage the lawman. There was only one course in his book: Stick to the trail.

At noon of the day Kirk Jordan and Joan Hutchinson were married in Santa Fe, Farrow and Curly jogged into Eph Gowan's ranch yard. They were fagged and hungry, and they needed water. For all his determination, the sheriff was on the point of giving up.

Gowan met them cagily, having little to say. He invited them to water their broncs, however; and while Farrow and the rancher talked, the deputy led the horses down to the tank.

He came back shortly, a discovery in his face which he revealed by striving for elaborate casualness. So pressing was it that he made little bones of accosting Farrow in an undertone. Gabe broke off his talk with Gowan to glance sharply at Curly, in irritation.

"What?" he growled, in answer to a mutter he did not catch.

"I said they's half-a-dozen calfskins dryin' over the corral fence out back," the deputy whispered sibilantly.

Gowan, watching the pair like a hawk, did not catch these words. By no sign did Farrow give away the electric shock which ran over him. He was not one to grab at straws. Neither was he prone to overlook the slightest chance.

"Get a look at 'em?"

"Well—they're brindles. Gowan's Injun was foolin' around out there. I didn't want to show too much curiosity."

Farrow nodded briefly.

"Reckon this was a purty nice place at one time, Gowan," he resumed, looking around.

Gowan did not draw easy. He grunted: "Yeah," and let it go at that.

Farrow strolled to the corner of the house. His eye ran down the yard curiously. Sure enough, there were the drying calfskins flung over a corral-pole. Gabe promptly forgot the amenities. He started for the corral, the light of purpose in his eye.

"Where yuh goin'?" Gowan called after him, gruffly.

"Not very far."

Gowan came off the porch as though spurred. He disregarded Curly, who stared at him watchfully. Gowan speedily saw the sheriff's object. He yelled:

"Straight Tongue!"

The dark-faced Apache showed his head above a wagon bed. He took in the situation at a glance.

He was nearer the corral than Farrow. With lithe, slouching stride he made for the drying skins.

"Here!" the lawman called, warningly. "Jest leave them hides where they be!"

The Indian did not so much as spare him a glance. He was pulling the calfskins off the fence, rolling them together preparatory to taking them away.

Farrow, his hatchet face flashing, was at his side in a moment. He laid a rough hand on the bundle under Straight Tongue's arm.

"Reckon I want to look at them hides, feller!"

"No. Can't have 'um," the Apache muttered.

"By God, I will have a look! . . . Gowan! Tell this redskin to lay off, if he knows what's good fer him," Farrow flung over his shoulder, loudly. At the same time, he began to tug at the bundle of hides.

Straight Tongue hung on to his bundle for a brief moment of struggle. Then suddenly he let go. Farrow staggered back, the skins in his grasp. Before he could recover, the Apache lunged into

129

him heavily. Farrow stumbled and went down rolling. The bundle of hides flew in the opposite direction.

While Farrow was straightening himself out, the Indian snatched up the hides and started away with them.

Farrow let out a squall of baffled wrath. Still on his knees, one hand on the ground, he went for his six-gun with the other.

"Here!" Eph Gowan bellowed. "You shoot that Injun an' I'll flatten yuh out!"

Farrow, however, was seeing red. He found time for one snapshot, the slug ricocheting off a corral post with a scream. Then Gowan was on him. His kick sent the lawman's gun flying. Then Farrow was on his feet and the two faced each other belligerently. Curly came running up, gun in hand. But he was not of the stuff which takes command; he only stood by while the recriminations flew above his head.

"Yo're goin' purty far, Gowan!" the sheriff flung out. "It's the law yo're buckin' now, I'll have yuh remember!"

"The hell with yore kind of law," old Eph told him defiantly. "If I hadn't stopped yuh, yuh'd have sunk lead in that Injun an' there'd been hell to pay!"

"There'll be hell to pay anyway, if yuh don't git him back here with them hides!" Farrow flared, his rage mounting as he perceived how neatly he had been defeated. "I'm havin' a look at 'em an' there ain't no two ways 'bout it!"

"Chop that kind of talk with me! Why should I show you or any man anythin' I don't happen to want to!"

"I reckon yuh know what I'm after, Gowan! I'm warnin' yuh—either I get a look at the brand on them brindle calfskins, or it'll go hard with yuh!"

"How'll it go with me?" Eph tossed back, bluntly. "What can yuh do?"

"Gowan, I don't aim to bandy words with yuh. Trot that Injun out here with them hides!" was the lawman's ultimatum.

"No!" came back the flinty refusal.

Farrow's grey-shot brows twitched. He did not otherwise move.

"Yuh won't meet me fair an' square in the open, Gowan?"

"Not that way, nor any other way!" Eph hurled back, with a pretense of fine wrath.

Without more words, Farrow wheeled away. His face was set and grim. He made a gesture to Curly, took the reins of his own bronc, and swinging aboard, turned and went jogging away from the ranch in the desert basin.

"Dang it, Gabe!" Curly burst out, some minutes later. "Them was our hides, shore's shootin'! What'll yuh do now?"

"I'm headin' fer Hutchinson's Ladder spread,"

Farrow bit out dourly. "Reckon there ain't much doubt them're the hides we want. If that's the case, they're as good that way as any way; an' we'll git 'em yet."

"How'll yuh do it?"

"Wal, I reckon Cole Hutchinson'll be as interested in seein' hides with the J Bar burned onto 'em as I am. I'll ask him fer a posse till this business is squared."

Before Curly and Farrow had gone a couple of miles, a Ladder puncher spotted them and rode forward. It was Len Decker.

"Wal, Farrow, how yuh makin' out?"

"I'll manage," the lawman returned.

Decker's eyes glinted. "Sounds like yuh had somethin'," he commented, encouragingly.

His manner was so smooth that a moment later Farrow found himself revealing what he had learned. Decker knew all about the hides he was seeking.

The latter's jaw dropped as the sheriff proceeded. "I'll be damned!" he ejaculated. "Gowan had them calf hides all the time? It'll put him in a tough spot, as well as Jordan, if yuh can prove that!"

Farrow jerked a nod.

"That's why the Injun tried to run a bluff on me," he agreed.

Decker pondered. "What yuh aimin' to do next?" he queried.

"I'm puttin' it up to Cole Hutchinson."

"Unh-uh." The puncher frowned, shaking his head. "Nothin' in that. Cole believes in walkin' wide of them redskins of Gowan's. He won't do nothin'."

"Redskins? There wasn't but one of 'em there!" Decker looked at the lawman pityingly. "Farrow, Gowan's got a couple dozen or more of them wolves at his beck an' call."

Farrow's face fell. "By Godfrey, I won't let Gowan run a blazer on me that way—or any other man! He's got them incriminatin' calf hides, an' I'm goin' to have 'em!"

Decker's visage fell into lines of craft. He pretended to hesitate, then declared:

"Danged if I don't see things yore way, myself. But Cole ain't the man to tackle, Farrow, you listen to me. Buck's the man yuh want. He'll git yuh some action pronto!"

"Where is Buck?"

"Wal—he said he was ridin' to Beartrack. I'll side yuh if yo're goin' there."

They set out without ado. It was midafternoon when they dropped down into the canyon. Reaching the crossing, they found Buck Hutchinson idling in Broke Hazen's bar. His glance traveled over the lawman without interest, as Farrow entered; but he straightened up on Len Decker's appearance. Curly had been left outside with the horses.

Decker and Farrow went directly to Buck.

"Hutchinson," said the sheriff, "come outside with us. I got some news fer yuh."

Buck came, his manner noncommittal. But his indifference dropped from him like a cloak when Gabe told his story.

"By God, I been lookin' for something like this a long while!" he burst out. "It couldn't fall out any neater! If we play our cards right, it'll not only spell aces an' eights for Gowan and Kirk Jordan, but it'll make a clean sweep of these damned Apaches too!"

Farrow showed irritation at Buck's assumption of authority. But he was as determined as the other that something decisive should be done. He passed it over for the time being.

"Can yuh gather 'nough of the Ladder crowd to help me lay hands on them hides?" he demanded, bluntly.

Buck grinned wolfishly.

"I not only can, but will. But we don't need to depend on the Ladder alone. There's a lot of cowmen in this country who'll be only too glad to get a crack at that rattler's den!"

Farrow hesitated. "Wal—"

Buck thrust his face close to the lawman's, his jaw pugnacious.

"Don't go stallin', Farrow! When it gets around what's been goin' on, it won't be so healthy for you if you keep such things to yourself!"

"Won't be so healthy fer some others, if we start a 'Pache uprisin', neither!"

"Don't worry," Buck bit off. "There won't be anythin' like that. We'll saw it off before it gets started!"

He wheeled away to step in the bar. His loud call brought several men in from the office side of Hazen's hotel. With swift, impassioned words, Buck Hutchinson revealed what was afoot.

"How 'bout it?" he challenged. "Any of you gents who don't want to ride against Gowan's nest of sidewinders?"

Those who didn't, failed to declare themselves. Ten minutes later, a group of nearly a dozen started away from Beartrack, grim of visage and heavily armed.

When they had climbed up out of the canyon, Buck Hutchinson turned to front them. It was plain that he had taken charge.

"Breen an' Henderson an' McGraw," he picked these men out; "you boys ride south and swing through the ranches along Rock Creek. Gather up every man you can, and ride for Castle Rock. We'll all meet there by sundown. . . . Rest of us'll hit the ranches to the north of the canyon. Make dang sure no fool punchers go ridin' the country with the news. We don't want Gowan or his Indians to get a smell of this before we're ready to strike! Got that?"

They had it. Within a matter of minutes they were on their way, the righteous wrath of the pioneer burning in every man.

The alarm spread through the Beartrack ranches with amazing speed. Men answered the call as if it were a call to repel invaders of their country.

With the sun hanging low in the west, a grim-faced crowd of men began to gather at Castle Rock, on the desert's edge. The posse had grown to more than two score by the time Buck Hutchinson and Gabe Farrow arrived there.

The lawman's eyes widened in frank surprise. He began to ask himself what he had started, and whether it might not get out of his grasp. Then his lips twisted ruefully. He had already lost control of the range forces. Though men deferred to him as a limb of the law, it was Buck Hutchinson who swayed them with hoarse, hot words; he who would control their actions.

"Boys," Buck bellowed, standing up in his stirrups, and fronting the sea of stern faces, "for years Eph Gowan's sheltered a nest of snakes and cow-killers! Them Apaches are worse than snakes—they'll turn on us all, the first real chance they get. Farrow, here, has got the goods on 'em at last. There ain't no doubt they stole those calves that Kirk Jordan branded! This is our chance to square for that—and make a clean sweep of this range, so's a man can live in peace! Are you with me?"

A deep-throated growl was his answer. A few minutes later, the armed posse was riding through the twilight in the direction of Eph Gowan's desert basin.

15

Curly edged over alongside Farrow and lowered his voice to mutter: "Pretty much of a posse, here, to help us collect half-a-dozen calf hides!"

Gabe's expression was serious.

"I'll see to it that nothin' goes wrong," was his response, as much to reassure himself as anything.

"Why, hell!" Curly burst out, at that. "Yuh won't be able to handle this bunch. We ain't doin' nothin' but servin' Hutchinson for an excuse to do his dirty work!"

Farrow put on a fierce look, and only said, "We'll see!"

The sun set in an angry red sky, and a murky dusk swam up out of the sage. It would be dark before the posse reached Gowan's place, but Buck Hutchinson appeared in no hurry. He recounted in a dogged tone to anyone who would listen the many crimes of Gowan's Apaches, declaring they should have been wiped out long ago.

Farrow stood it till it got on his nerves.

"See here, Hutch," he broke in, then. "This sounds mighty like a war-talk yo're puttin' on. Don't make any mistake—calf hides is what we're after, an' nothin' else!"

Hutchinson stared at him insolently, his eyeballs glinting in the last light of the sky.

"What'll you be doin' if Gowan refuses to hand 'em over, and backs it up with a bunch of redskins?" he queried thinly.

"Wal—" Farrow hadn't considered that. "Reckon that's why we brought the boys along. But we'll give Gowan a chance to come through first, an' get tough afterward."

Hutchinson snorted in what might have been contempt, and slanted a sly smile in the direction of a crony. Farrow caught that scornful by-play and the hot blood rushed into his face, but he said nothing more, only clamping his jaws together with determination.

Darkness thickened. Talk died away.

They entered Gowan's desert basin, the sand muffling the sounds of their progress.

Eph Gowan's ranch house presented a mild appearance: a black and silent box-like shape in the gloom. A light burned inside, making a single daub of color in the open door.

The posse spread as it neared, presenting a broad line toward the house. It was Farrow who advanced to the porch, Hutchinson not far behind him.

Farrow called out, gruffly: "Hello, Gowan!"

For a moment, silence answered the call. Then there was a stir inside. The light went out. Gowan's harsh answer came:

"Wal, what yuh want, Farrow?"

"I come back after them calf hides, and I'm goin' to have 'em!"

"Yuh are, like hell!"

Buck Hutchinson listened to this exchange with gritted teeth. He had a personal interest in seeing those telltale hides turned over to the law. Suddenly, sharply, he cut across the talk:

"All right, Gowan! We got the place surrounded. Trot out them hides in a hurry!"

Gowan could read a deadly threat when he heard it. Yet his retort was instantaneous.

"Go to hell, Hutchinson!"

There was the harsh whine of a snarl in Buck's throat now. "All right, boys—!"

Farrow jerked out: "Hold on, Hutch!"

But before anything could happen, an unearthly, blood-curdling screech rent the air. It was the Apache war-cry, coming from near at hand. The hair lifted on every scalp in the posse. Hands gripped rifles until the knuckles whitened.

There was a moment of terrible silence.

It was broken by a sharp crack from the direction of Gowan's corrals. A nervous posseman answered it, firing instantly in that direction. Then hell broke loose.

"Gang up and smoke 'em out of the corrals!" Buck Hutchinson roared.

There was a rush in that direction. Every man was fighting as fiercely as he knew how, with the disadvantage of enveloping darkness.

Apache yells rang out at intervals. For whatever purpose the Indians had collected here, they were ready for anything. Their carbines barked viciously, never from precisely the same position the second time.

Gabe Farrow was throwing lead along with the others. Bitter as this dose was for him, he took Gowan's defiance of his demands at face value. There was nothing else to be done. If Gowan hoped to hide behind a bulwark of red allies, he must be blasted out.

Contrary to Buck's hopes, however, the struggle was not briefly decided. Plainly the Apaches were as determined as these ranchers and cowboys.

More than once, when the possemen rushed the corrals or the saddle shed in force, they met with hand-to-hand resistance.

The fighting flamed into stark savagery. It was impossible to herd the Apaches in any given direction, however; nor could they be laid hold of, squirming out of the firmest grip with the agility of eels.

Of a sudden there was a rush in the direction of the water tank. Buck bawled:

"They're makin' a break! Stop 'em before they reach their broncs!"

Easier ordered than done! Carbines snarled spitefully in the face of a withering blast of rifle-fire. There was a swirl and a rush, and the Indians broke and swooped away like the desert hawks they were.

Curly yelled: "Gripes! There must be better'n a couple dozen o' them devils!"

The posse, at a loss, milled in darkness while each man sought his pony, or, failing that, anything that would serve as a mount.

"After 'em, boys!" Buck Hutchinson yelled harshly.

"What about them hides?" Gabe Farrow hurled at him.

It brought Buck up short. He swung toward Gowan's house, strode forward with driving purpose.

"Hey there, Gowan!"

His answer was a burst of gunfire. Old Eph evidently had the house barricaded and meant to stick to the last.

"Gowan!"

"Spit it out!" Gowan snarled, furiously.

"Are you comin' acrost with them hides, or are we smokin' you out of there?"

The answer was more lead. Gabe Farrow grunted from the impact of a slug which glanced off his cartridge-belt, tearing out the loops.

"Last warnin', Gowan!" There was a wicked recklessness in the words.

"The hell with yuh!" Eph bawled, wildly. "Them hides went with the Injuns, if yuh want to know! But come ahead an' see for yerself!" he added, boldly.

Buck cursed luridly.

"He's tellin' the truth," he ripped out, whirling on Farrow. "Don't forget, them hides would get him into a jackpot as well as Kirk Jordan!"

"I ain't forgettin'!" Gabe retorted.

"So, what do you think of it now?"

All Farrow's stubbornness came out of him in a rush.

"Get them hides!"

Hutchinson whirled toward his bronc, gathering his bulky, squat body as he did so.

"Right into it, boys!" he bellowed. "Our job ain't done yet!"

They turned away from Gowan's place with scant ceremony.

"Where'll them 'Paches head fer?" Curly fired out.

"Reservation," Buck grunted.

It gave Farrow pause. To hound the Indians to their last refuge would be doing more than he had bargained for. Chastising a few renegades was one thing. To barge into the reservation itself meant involving every warrior there.

But there was no other course open. The actions of the Apaches constituted a grave obstruction of justice, or so Farrow saw it. He meant to see that the law was observed first, then square with the Indian Department the best way he could.

Some of the posse had been left without mounts. But Eph Gowan had some extra horses in his pasture. These were roped and snaked out, the saddles yanked off the dead broncs and cinched on them. The posse swung away into the darkness.

There was a different air about them than before. They had smelled powder. Some of them bore the marks of slugs. They were deaf to their peril; intent only in meting out vengeance to the Apaches.

Hutchinson growled: "We'll head for the reservation and count on findin' the devils there. Should get there an hour before dawn. That'll give us time to figure our play."

Farrow put in: "Look, now, Hutch! I ain't aimin' to stampede them redskins. What I'm after's them hides!"

"D'you think I ain't?" Buck snapped back.

"Wal, there's a right way of goin' about this, an' a wrong way—"

"You keep yore ways to yoreself!" Buck rasped, on edge with fury and disappointment. "You've had two plays at gettin' them hides, Farrow, and muffed 'em both. Now I'm takin' charge!"

"Reckon we'll see about that!" Gabe muttered.

Buck jammed his bronc close to the lawman's.

"What was that?" he blazed.

Farrow chose to maintain silence.

Threading the pine forest and crossing canyons,

they came at last to what Buck said was the reservation boundary.

"Keep an eye peeled. No tellin' what we're liable to run into from now on."

Steadily they drilled on. The Indians had set up their village in a shallow canyon some miles in from the reservation boundary. Slowly and carefully the posse drew up on it.

Not a man but felt a spirit alien to his experience when they drew up at last on the brink of the canyon and looked over and down. The Apache pueblo showed no sign of life. Not even a stray mongrel barked. There was only the lonely yip-yip-yip of a coyote far away across the hills.

"We got to make this short an' sweet," said Buck, as the possemen gathered behind him. "We'll surround the place, and when the first streaks get bright enough to see, ride in. Herd every danged Apache back toward the center. Then we'll haul out the bucks and settle this business!"

There was prolonged murmuring as plans were perfected. Then one by one, horsemen faded into the shadows. Silence returned to the canyon, and the appearance of peace.

A faint thread of light raveled the eastern sky. The tear widened, the light strengthening. Suddenly, on the outskirts of the pueblo, there was a cowboy yell. The thunder of hooves grew.

As quickly as a disturbed ant-heap begins

to boil, the pueblo sprang to life. There were a few high-pitched war cries above the crackle of gunfire from the posse, but no wails. Women and children darted thither and yon in silence. The bucks and braves put in an appearance, fiercely ready. Bow-strings twanged. Carbines exploded. A fiercely commanding figure sprang to the fore, waving to his men. This was the call to battle!

Gabe Farrow sucked in his breath, a sudden apprehension knifing through him. There would be no parleying here. Not only did they face bitter conflict, but it looked as though they had bit off more than they could chew.

The Apaches ran here and there confusingly in the half-light. Despite Buck Hutchinson's authoritative yells, there was little that could be done with them. Suddenly a naked, copper-skinned horde of demons mounted on the fleetest of horses swirled into the open before the pueblo.

Far from hesitating, they swept straight toward the posse with the force of a battering-ram. The two bodies met, Apache and posseman coming together with solid impact. War cries curdled the morning. Guns crashed.

A long moment the issue was in doubt. Then slowly the posse was hurled back. Punchers broke away and fled, each followed by several Indians. Buck Hutchinson found himself among the fugitives. Gabe Farrow was not far away, making tracks as fast as he could.

"My Gawd!" Curly burst out. "Them wolves are on the prod fer fair! There won't be no holdin' 'em now! They'll tear through the country like a range fire!"

Farrow knew it was so. So did Buck. But all the latter could think of was that in the face of this surprising resistance by the Apaches, he had failed to lay hands on the evidence which he had hoped would damn Kirk Jordan on this range for good and all.

16

Swinging back to his herd from the stage-station, Kirk as yet had no great fears. There had been a dozen Apache up-risings in the past five years; never as serious as they sounded. But remembering the stark conditions of ten years ago, men continued to react automatically to these scares.

Usually the Apaches went beserk for a day, wreaked their bloodthirsty wrath on an out-lying squatter's ranch or two and then faded into the mountain fastnesses, where army scouts were forced patiently to seek them out and persuade them to return to a quieter way of life.

As for Joan's being in any danger, Kirk didn't believe it for a minute. The Indians were coming to understand, by bitter experiences, that stages must remain inviolate; that more than anything else, their destruction called down sharp, telling retaliation upon their heads.

Besides that, she was the daughter of Cole Hutchinson. Old as he was, he was a power in the desert country. Even Eph Gowan's Apaches refrained from open acts of violence against him and his. No, Kirk thought—Joan will be as safe on the stage as she would be in Santa Fe.

He realized, however, that he was attempting

to persuade himself to this effect. The knowledge would not let him rest.

By the time he reached the steers he had made up his mind. Whatever might happen, the trail-pace of the cattle was too slow for him.

He told the two punchers briefly what he had heard at the stage-station. Their faces went blank, but they gave no sign that the news affected them.

"You'll make out all right," he told them. "I'm going to push ahead, just to be on the safe side. If there's any trouble up the trail, you'll hear from me."

"Shore, Jordan," said one.

He gave them terse instructions, then swung his bronc's head toward the west and exerted pressure with his knees. The pony jogged away from the billowing, golden dust and headed out across the illimitable sagebrush plain.

The land was broken by long swells. It was not long before Kirk had dropped the herd behind, out of sight. He rode with all his senses keyed; for there was something in the mere suggestion of an Apache up-rising that no man could wholly ignore.

The desert was as silent and empty under the ardent blast of the sun as though it had never known disturbance of any kind. Above a distant line of rocky hills a hawk circled majestically. Nearer a coyote appeared between brush clumps, gazed for a moment, then faded from sight.

Yet the very atmosphere of the afternoon made Kirk push ahead more briskly. There seemed something sinister hovering behind the very benignity of the sky, some threat he could not read to its end, but whose warning he understood thoroughly.

"The stage'll roll across this country at a good, round clip," he murmured, trying to ease the tautness of his strung nerves. "It'd be a miracle if the Indians just happened to so much as get a flash of it."

But he could not wholly deceive himself thus. Apaches, he knew well enough, had the stealth and cunning of the desert animals themselves. After generations of the hardest kind of living in this iron land, from which nothing could drive them, they seemed less human men than desert denizens in the shape of men. It was entirely within the scope of possibility, should the thought come to life, for them to lie in wait for the stage.

His glance, sharpened with anxiety, ran constantly ahead along the stage trail—a faint, open track threading the brush for miles, like a white ribbon carelessly flung down. As far as he could see, nothing broke the surface of the barren land. But there were the long swells to be considered. At no time could he see farther ahead than two, three, perhaps four miles. The circumstance forced him into a series of anxieties, while he rode from one ridge-crest to another. Each arrival was a nerve-stretching moment, while he had his look beyond.

He was far ahead of the slowly moving steers now—ten, a dozen miles. Still he had seen nothing whatever to excite his worry in the slightest. A sensible man, he told himself, would turn back, rejoin the stock, and proceed in a reasonable fashion. But everything else fell away before the fact that Joan was on that stage. That she was Cole Hutchinson's daughter meant nothing. She was his wife; dearer to him than he had dreamed anything would ever be.

The sun arched down the west while he thrust on. It changed gradually in color, losing its golden brilliance, taking a reddish tinge which communicated itself to the hills, the air. Another half-hour would bring the sunset.

Still Kirk drove on, forced forward by an impulse he could scarcely understand himself.

He could not hope to reach home tonight. There were still fifty or sixty miles to be covered. If the steers got there two days from today, it was as much as could be expected. So Kirk was thinking, when suddenly he jerked in on the reins. Some warning of disaster wrapped itself about his chest like an iron band and his blood turned to ice.

Rising over a little swell in the trail, he had ridden almost upon the grisly thing which lay there in plain sight.

A burnt wagon, smouldering still, tinging the clean air with a charred odor lay all but destroyed in a heap of heat-twisted metal scraps. Face down on the ground beside it lay a dead man. When Kirk saw what had been done to him, he jerked his eyes away with a shuddering effort.

Another man lay half-a-dozen yards away, his clothes torn, powder stains darkening his skin, his eyes staring and glassy. The four stage-horses lay in a senseless heap, still entangled in their harness. Their throats had been cut.

The one item of intelligence which penetrated to Kirk's brain in that terrible moment of stunned numbness was that Joan was nowhere in sight. His thoughts repeated that stupidly until its meaning sank home.

Gone! Joan gone! What did that mean? Then he shied away from the inevitable inference, the only conceivable answer to that question. Something in him revolted.

"No! It can't be!" he groaned hoarsely. "They wouldn't take her away—!"

But all the protestation in the world failed to alter the facts. Stiffly he slid down from his pony's back and moved here and there in the light of dusk, searching thoroughly, dreading what he might find. When he was done he knew for certain: Joan was nowhere near this spot. She must have been taken away.

It spelled a fate worse than mere speedy death.

There was an element of horror in what might be happening to her even at this minute. Sweat burst out on Kirk's brow, his temples, and ran down his face.

"God!"

It was a more fervent prayer than many a copious and well-chosen flow of words. But Kirk did not leave it at that. Bitterly he forced his wits to work, to indicate to him how he was to proceed at such a time.

"I can't track the devils!" he burst out. "They'd see to that, if dark wasn't coming on!"

A new thought knifed into his consciousness—Eph Gowan. The man had a closer contact with the Apaches than anyone Kirk had any knowledge of on the desert. It was a forlorn hope that he might extend anything in the nature of help, even at that. Folly to suppose that Indians, on the eve of a savage out-break against the hated white men, would allow any slightest inkling of their intentions to reach the ear of one of the enemy race.

But it was Kirk's sole hope, and he was quick to realize as much. It was just possible that he could persuade Gowan to act before it was too late.

He galvanized into action, swinging into the hull on the run. His bronc raced away from the scene of the massacre as though pursued by demons. But that was a sheer display of nerves, in the face of an all-night ride. Before he had gone a hundred yards, Kirk mastered his frenzy of haste and forced the pony down to a moderate pace.

He drilled on, while darkness swam up out of the brush and the stars came out, cold, pitiless, far-off. He was scarcely conscious of the ride itself, only of its interminable drawing-out, his bleak thoughts circling and closing in like a ghostly Indian attack on his sanity.

Had he married Joan only a few days ago, to lose her now, and in so cruel a manner? Something at the core of his being revolted against that, holding out a thin hope that was little more than a formality.

Time dragged. The wind of his own speed tugged at his face, his lean lips and slitted eyes. It must have been near midnight that he suddenly hauled in again, jerking the bronc down.

He had heard nothing. It was rather the evidence of his nostrils that gave him pause. Again that rank, pungent odor of burning!

Kirk pushed ahead with slow caution. The smell came stronger now. There was little light; the moon would not rise until early morning. But by the faint luminous star-glow he made out heaps here and there in the trail. The reading, after what he had already seen, was plain. This was another burnt wagon. A ranch equipage, probably, belonging to some small outfit back in the hills.

Cold rage clamped his heart. With murder and rapine stalking the desert, he would have asked nothing better than to come head-on into the coppery-skinned demons who were responsible. He would have been content with the outcome, whatever it was.

The attack on the stage had been terrible enough. With this additional barbarity, what hope could there be in any sane mind for Joan's safe survival?

Cold and grim as steel, Kirk pulled around the spot and hurled on. Eph Gowan was his objective now. Nothing must stand between. . . .

It was a badly beaten bronc that shuffled into Gowan's desert basin shortly before dawn. All the raking with spurs which Kirk had done during the last half-hour had been of no avail. The horse was done up.

Kirk flung out of the saddle and made the steps in three tremendous strides. He hammered on the door-post with his gun, at the same time calling into the opening:

"Gowan! Eph Gowan!"

Morning silence held the building in unbroken grip. This might have been the home of the dead. Desperation splashed over Kirk's already full cup. Was it possible that Gowan was away at this time—perhaps in some connection with his Indians?

He had stepped inside, peering into shadows.

He turned back now, for a look at the corrals. In the moment of his emergence, he spotted a fleeting movement at the house-corner. A second later Gowan himself stepped into view.

"Hullo," he said, somewhat vaguely. "That you, Jordan? I thought—"

Kirk sprang to him. Pale green light was spreading in the east; they were scarcely more than recognizable to each other, their eyes luminous.

"Gowan, there's hell to pay and I need your help!"

Eph stared at him, arrested for that moment.

"I got troubles of my own, Jordan—" he began, grumpily.

"The stage was attacked by Apaches seventy miles east—driver and guard killed—and Gowan, the devils carried Cole Hutchinson's girl off!"

Gowan's eyes glazed. Kirk could feel the hardness of him as he slowly stiffened.

"Hutchinson's girl, huh?" He didn't bother to add any insincerities. He was not sorry.

Kirk jerked out: "I've got to get her back! Gowan, have you a ghost of a notion where they'd take her?"

Gowan said: "No," instantly and solidly.

Kirk's features congested. "Dammit, Gowan; forget your crazy hatred of Cole Hutchinson for a minute! This girl never did you any harm! Now the Apaches have got her—God knows what they intend to do with her! Can't you understand, man? She's a white woman—"

"Yeh, I get it." Eph was brusque. His eyes bored into Kirk. "Are yuh shore they got 'er?"

"I was told at a stage-station that she was on the wagon! When I found it, burnt, the horses killed, she wasn't there. Isn't that plain enough?"

Kirk's impatience was boiling in him now; but he knew he must handle Gowan carefully.

Eph nodded woodenly. "Looks like there can't be no mistake." He left it at that, spitting and looking away.

Kirk could stand no more. Words spilled out of him with savage force:

"Gowan, where have they taken her? You know!" he proceeded without softening the accusation in the slightest. "You must know! If there's one man hand-in-glove with the Apaches in all New Mexico and Arizona, it's you! . . . Out with it!"

Gowan eyed him oddly. Even his words had an odd ring: "By Godfrey, Jordan—I b'lieve yuh mean that!"

Kirk was helpless with rage and chagrin. "Mean it!" he echoed crazily. "You know damned well I mean it! . . . Gowan, for God's sake think. Are you a red devil too, under your white skin?" He put all the scathing contempt he could muster into the question.

Eph's visage went grey.

"Hyere!" he broke in harshly. "There ain't no call to be talkin' that way! I tell yuh I dunno where them Injuns might be takin' the girl—if they got 'er at all!"

Kirk groaned. He had lost. It might well be true, what Gowan said. There were some things Indians would never allow any white man to know. Certainly the Apaches had a sufficient grievance against Cole Hutchinson to determine to strike at him; but they might well do it without involving Gowan in any manner.

"To think she's been my wife less than a week—" he got out, brokenly.

Gowan froze, staring. "What?" he demanded incredulously.

"We were married in Santa Fe," Kirk explained, dully. "It doesn't mean anything now—"

Gowan swallowed with difficulty. "Yuh mean—yuh married Hutchinson's girl, Jordan?"

"Yes—"

It meant plenty to old Eph. He was the one who had virtually steered Kirk Jordan into Hutchinson's country to be a thorn in his side. The scheme had succeeded admirably. But to hear from his own lips that Kirk had married Joan Hutchinson was a staggerer. Gowan saw his revenge more complete than he had ever dreamed.

"Does Cole Hutchinson know about thi—?"

"No. He'll never need to, now."

Gowan's tone was gruff. "Mebby, Jordan. Mebby. I'm willin' to help all I can. . . ."

Kirk's bowed head came up with a jerk.

"What are you talking about?"

Eph's stare was steady. "Do yuh know where old Fort Rader is—'bandoned military post, forty miles southwest in the White Mountains?"

"I could find it," was Kirk's grim response.

"Wal—that's where the Apaches hole up after they been out raisin' hell. Straight Tongue dropped the information one time—"

"You mean that Joan is there—at old Fort Rader?"

"I dunno." Gowan was half-confused, dogged. "Mebby—an' mebby not. But yuh want to know where to look, Jordan. If yo're askin' me, I'd say—take a look there!" Eph jerked his head for emphasis. "If yuh don't get wind of the girl there, yuh won't ever find 'er anywhere."

Kirk believed him. He had no choice. There was little question that Gowan knew what he was talking about. He was simply putting it in such a way that it could not be pinned on him in the event of a tragedy he suspected but would not name.

Kirk yanked the saddle off his own spent bronc and threw it on one of Gowan's ponies. He pulled away from the barren basin without another word having passed his lips. His spurs were red before he had gone a mile.

17

A wild and terrible day followed the raid on the Apache pueblo. The berserk braves ranged far and wide with incredible speed, carrying death and fury across the sage.

Racing away after the failure of their hopes, the posse was effectually scattered. A witless fear of inhuman violence and savagery lived in the minds of these men. It was not until he knew himself safe from instant retribution that Buck Hutchinson began to think consecutively again.

He found himself riding down a slope on the far side of which he spied several other riders. Advancing cautiously before he hailed, he found them to be a trio of Ladder punchers who had been at Beartrack at the time the posse started out, and whom Buck had brought along.

They met him with wolfish grins.

"Still in one piece, eh, Buck?" was the callous greeting of one.

They talked it over in short, pungent phrases. It was plain that Buck had something on his mind.

"Reckon there'll be hell to pay tonight," he growled, finally. "But why leave it to chance for lightning to strike in the right place?"

They gazed at him, uncertain of his meaning.

"What yuh drivin' at?"

"Kirk Jordan and his rustlin' pal are the ones I'm thinkin' about!" Buck ground out. "If we could be sure the 'Paches would pay their outfit a visit, it'd be okay. But—" He broke off with a significant inflection, and a sinister twist of his lips.

"So what yuh thinkin' of—?"

Buck became crafty. "We'll wait till dark. There's four of us. What's the matter with makin' sure of Jordan and his pal our own way?"

A chorus of muttered approval met the suggestion.

"By God, I never had no use fer Jordan, anyway!" one burst out, harshly. "An' that goes fer Pecos Johnson too."

Buck wasted no time driving home their determination. "Let's get into it!" he grated, pulling his bronc around.

They went racing over the hills, not unlike Apaches themselves, a truculence in their bearing. It was now early afternoon, however; there must be a delay before they could act. They rode on to an outlying Ladder line camp and cooked themselves a meal, which they wolfed down with ravenous appetite.

The afternoon waned. Buck, strolling in front of the cabin, rolled and smoked a meditative cigarette. Finally he tossed it away, and turning, hitched up his belt.

"Time to get goin', boys," he announced. "It'll

be after dusk before we reach Jordan's J Bar."

They started on. Sunset was a lurid splash of crimson across the west. Gradually it faded and the concealing shadows mustered. It was under cover of thickening night that the four dropped into the Upper Basin and began to work toward the ranch Kirk and Pecos had built on its slope.

"No noise," Buck warned. "No clickin' stones or bustin' brush. We don't want to give no warning. Keep an eye peeled to make sure we don't barge into some cruisin' 'Paches, too."

But they felt reasonably safe. Had the Indians preceded them here, they would inevitably catch the scent of charred logs, the bloody stench of slain J Bar steers.

The cabin in the open had a noncommittal appearance when they paused in the edge of the pines and had their look.

"Both asleep," was Buck's opinion. "Or else they ain't got in yet. . . . We'll strike sudden, ridin' down there and settin' a match to that cabin. We better drill the ponies in the corral, too, to make it look like 'Pache work."

His words were low, tense, guttural. The others were in the grip of a suppressed ferocity as well, whipping up their hatred in preparation for the violence they meant to wreak.

"Nick, you take the corrals. The rest'll ride in circles an' whoop while I set the fire. Blast down anybody that shows! . . . Let's go!"

They broke from cover like ghostly specters. Streaking toward the cabin, they jerked out guns. In a moment, ugly red flares were stabbing the velvet night, slugs slamming into the pine logs.

To their amazement, almost without any delay between, their fire was answered with brisk savagery from the cabin. A six-gun stuttered its fierce challenge. Then the deeper *spang* of a rifle ripped the night.

The raiders were brought up short, expecting no such resistance as this. The fire from the cabin was not only hot: it was accurate. Buck's hat was twitched away, a jagged tear in the brim. One of the punchers let out a realistic howl as lead burned across his throat; another was struck by flying fragments of leather as a slug smashed his saddle horn.

"They was waitin' fer this!" an infuriated voice jerked out. "We don't stand a chance, Buck!"

Buck Hutchinson could have killed the man who not only burst into strident English, but used his name in the bargain. Little hope of passing themselves off as Apaches now!

Gritting his teeth, Buck threw himself into the attack with bitter fury. It did him little good. He never got anywhere near the cabin to set it ablaze. The puncher who had ridden toward the corrals circled back away, hanging onto a punctured forearm.

But their rage was up. For an hour they hovered

around the ranch, raking it with a brisk fire. The answer was judicious and effective. Pecos, alone as he was, had planned his defense in the event of just such an attack; and he had not planned amiss.

Long before midnight brought the soaring moon, Buck called off his men. Wrath all but choked him.

"Damn it all, we ain't got a chance here! But it ain't our fault. I lay it to Gabe Farrow. He was handed the charge against Jordan and Johnson, proof and all, and he botched it in fine style! Lord knows where he is now!"

Ruefully they turned their ponies' heads away from the Upper Basin and down the slopes. Little was said, for defeat rode with them. But Buck began to show signs of returning spirit when they drew near Eph Gowan's place.

"Gowan's as much to blame as anybody for what's happened!" he jerked out. "I say we give him what we was aimin' to give to Jordan! There won't be any Indians around his place now— they're all hittin' the war path, with their knives out for every white man in their way!"

The battered punchers were not so enthusiastic now, but they welcomed an opportunity to vent hate and chagrin on someone or something. They swung toward Gowan's ranch without demur.

Buck devised no elaborate approach this time. An ingrained brutality came out in him, lending him a force to which ordinarily he was a stranger. He jogged straight to Gowan's place and swung out of the saddle like a man with a task from which nothing could turn him.

"Gowan!" he called, harshly.

After a brief delay, Eph made his appearance in the door. He was alone. A rifle slanted in his grasp. Seeing who it was, without a word he started to raise the rifle.

A shot rang out as one of the punchers fired. Gowan's rifle twisted in his grasp and he dropped it as though it were hot.

Without slowing his stride, Buck marched forward, laid a heavy hand on old Eph and jerked him out. A thrust sent the old man spinning aside. Buck faced him, stark purpose in his blunt visage.

"Gowan, where's them hides Farrow wanted?"

Eph blew up, shaken by fury. For a moment he cursed Buck with the vehemence of a madman, and only broke off with the failure of his breath. "They ain't here!" he panted, at the end.

"Think it over, Gowan!" Buck warned, with deadly inflection. "It's them hides, or yours!"

"You be damned!" Gowan bawled. "I tell yuh—"

Buck turned heavily away. There was no theatrics in this. "Keep 'im out here," he growled to one of his men. Then he stepped in the house.

From the three downstairs rooms Buck dragged everything he could find that was inflammable.

He piled this in a heap in the kitchen. Picking up a coal-oil can then, he poured the liquid over the pile. Finally he struck a match and tossed it down.

There was a flicker, the blaze caught, and with a roar the oil-soaked mass burst into fierce conflagration.

Old Eph guessed what was afoot even before he was sure. He broke into wild recriminations, yelling until he was hoarse. A puncher pushed close and banged him over the head with the barrel of his Colt. Gowan choked and sprawled down. He wasn't out. It took all the effort in his withered body to bring himself to hands and knees. He started to crawl away.

One of the punchers made a coarse witticism.

Buck came out of the house, black and oily curls of smoke wreathing the door frame behind him. He was as grim and stern as rock.

"Drive Gowan's bronc in to the water tank," he rasped. "Shoot 'em there!"

The punchers turned to comply. If Gowan knew what was going on, he gave no sign, crawling doggedly away, bedraggled and whipped. Buck spared him little more than a glance. It didn't seem worth his while to kill the man. Gowan would have no choice but to leave this country now. That was enough.

Ten minutes later, Buck and his men rode across the desert basin in the direction of the

Ladder ranch. Behind them Gowan's house and shed were burning fiercely. An ominous roll of smoke welled from the spot and moved across the sands like a tattered banner.

Buck looked back once, as if to dwell on the small success he had achieved. He jerked his head in a brief nod, confirming something to himself.

"We'll serve Jordan that way someday," he let drop, a hint of bitterness in the words at the thought that they had been unable to do so tonight.

Darkness hid everything but that lurid torch.

It was not yet midmorning, the following day, when Cole Hutchinson stepped out of the Ladder ranch house and paused on the gallery as Len Decker came forward toward him. The cowman's mien was stern.

"What's goin' on, anyway?" he barked. "Where's Buck an' the boys?"

Decker seemed unwilling to meet his stabbing gaze.

"Wal—they're back, boss. Sawin' wood in the bunkhouse."

"What?"

The tone of that made Decker jump.

"Yeh, they didn't git in till round three o'clock this mornin'," he said hurriedly. "I ain't had a chance to talk to Buck yet."

"Wal, when the lazy pup comes to—" Cole broke off, his keen gaze focusing as a figure like a scarecrow came riding into the ranch yard. It was Eph Gowan. He had got a rack of bones somewhere. His clothes were in tatters. His eye sockets were deep. His big eyes burned with the fire of a maniac.

He saw Hutchinson. Limp and bedraggled as he was, sight of his ancient enemy put new life in him. Flinging out of the hull, he ran staggering forward, one clawed hand extended over his head.

"Hutchinson!" he screeched, beside himself with ungovernable passion. "Damn yore soul, yo're the hombre I want!"

Cole stood like an aged grey rock, staring at this sight from under craggy brows. His voice came in a grizzly rumble.

"Gowan, git off my ranch!"

It was plain that he was holding himself in check only with the bitterest effort.

"By God, I will—with you dead!"

Gowan was clawing for a six-gun he seemed too much beside himself to manage.

"Decker," Cole blazed, "throw this dang buzzard—"

"No yuh don't!" Eph whipped out. "I'm squarin' with yuh for years of dirty work, Hutchinson! It was you, drove me off the range till I lost my beef! You done me a thousand nasty tricks! You ordered them 'Paches stampeded, an' ordered my place burnt out! By God, I'll have yore heart or die tryin'!"

"What yuh blowin' about?" Cole flung at him, scathingly. "I dunno a thing 'bout yore danged Injuns, or burnin', or anything else. I always thought yuh'd go off yore head over there! Now yuh done it!"

"Lies!" Old Eph bellowed, his voice cracking. "But the Lord'll square with yuh, Hutchinson, if I don't!"

Cole snorted, the bitterness of years heating his veins.

"Yuh can't do nothin', yuh crazy bag o' bones!"

With a squall, Gowan rushed. His gun came out, wobbling this way and that, as he came. It exploded, and chips and chunks flew from the corner of the gallery as the slug went wild.

With a bellow, Cole shoved forward. He met Gowan with solid impact. The six-gun went flying out of Eph's grasp. Then they were at each other like wolves.

But Gowan was too far gone to put up any material resistance. With a violent effort, Cole flung him down. He stepped close, and raised his boot in a crushing gesture, but after a moment put it back to the ground. Eph struggled up on an elbow, his face ghastly with defeat.

"Yuh got me now, Hutchinson!" he croaked. "But yo're fightin' a bigger thing than me, an'

169

don't yuh forget it! A couple more years an' yuh won't have no more ranch than yuh left me!"

"Shut up!" Cole roared. "Git up on yore hocks an' take yoreself off! By Godfrey, I won't have carrion like you around!"

Gowan drew back swiftly as Cole made a threatening gesture with his quirt. Eph forgot his gun. He backed rapidly away, bile making his twisted visage inhuman.

"Yuh got the upper hand now, Hutchinson!" he quavered. "But I'll live to laugh at yuh—taunt yuh when the desert sweeps over yore head an' yuh ain't got a steer to yore name! Remember that!"

Cole's face grew black.

"Travel!" he blazed, ominously.

Gowan clawed up on his scarecrow mount, and, turning its head, kicked it in the ribs and rode from sight.

18

Kirk Jordan's face was grim, his thoughts grimmer, as he rode into the grey morning after pulling away from Eph Gowan's desert basin. The hooves of his pony hammered a wild tattoo as he drove it to greater and greater effort.

He knew in what direction old Fort Rader lay. The lay of the land had been described to him.

But would he find it soon enough? Was Joan already given over to the rage of the ruthless Apaches—mutilated, dead? There could be little doubt that the Indian outbreak traced back to the brave Buck Hutchinson's crowd had hung at the high fork of Feather Creek. The savages would direct their wrath in Cole Hutchinson's direction. It was possible they had known the cattleman's daughter was on the stage; that they had planned with fiendish ingenuity with the end in view of making the old man suffer through violence to his girl.

The logic of this drove the blood from Kirk's cheeks. If he was right, the Apaches would see to it that he never reached Joan's side. He knew this with the certainty of fate. It did not deter him.

The sun rose and began to climb. Kirk's choice of a mount had been a fortunate one. The pony drove steadily into the rising hills with a heart of iron. Lather flecked its jaws, for Kirk gave it little consideration. There were issues at stake more important than horseflesh.

Except for small game and an occasional deer, the pine slopes were empty of life. Mile after mile went by and Kirk saw no sign of human passage. He was not looking for trails. His sole object was to reach the abandoned military post in the shortest possible time. It was as though the very silence of the hills held him back. He strove ahead of the flying hooves under him, his keen glance taking note of landmarks.

The faces of the Apaches he had seen around Eph Gowan's place flitted through his mind, and his pulse hammered ever faster. What might they not be capable of? His one hope was that he still retained something of their good-will. Yet even with a white man whom they considered a friend, there remained something sinister in their dark nature.

The sun marked an hour past midday when he rode out on a rimrock and looked down into a timbered basin in the open hollow of which lay a scattering of tumble-down adobe buildings which he knew at once was Fort Rader.

Tiny figures moved down there. He caught gaudy patches of color which were the paint ponies in a corral. He had little doubt that he was seen already. But it was his intention to be seen. His only chance lay in hiding nothing, but in advancing openly, and openly making his request of the Indians there.

That Joan was held a prisoner below he had not the slightest doubt. Eph Gowan had been ashamed, it seemed, to admit that he knew anything of the Indians' intentions toward a white woman. But he had said without hesitation that Kirk would find the Apaches here. He had not been wrong.

The facts threw a sinister light over Gowan's own figure. Kirk knew that the lust for revenge against his ancient enemy bit into Gowan's heart like an acid. But that he should relegate his vengeance in this ghastly manner was enough to turn the blood cold. Kirk undeniably owed the man much. Yet he would never look at him again without sharp aversion.

He was forced to circle to get down off the rimrock. Half-an-hour served to bring him within three miles of the old fort, on lower ground. Still he had laid eyes on no moving figure near at hand. Despite his watchfulness, it came as a surprise when a hawk-faced, breech-clouted Indian materialized in his path to stand fifty yards ahead with upraised hand.

Kirk drew rein and stared. The fact that he had not been slain from ambush told him he was recognized. Yet he did not know this lean, ironwood brave by sight.

"Go back" was the latter's guttural order.

Kirk pushed his pony forward slowly and deliberately, keeping his eye fixed on the Indian. The other bore menacingly a carbine Kirk had little difficulty in recognizing as the weapon belonging to a stage guard.

"You know me? I am Kirk Jordan. I do not know you; but your brothers know me. Who are you?"

The Apache stared inscrutably out of a coppery mask. His lips barely moved: "You want to live? Go back!"

Kirk came on fearlessly.

"You will not tell me who you are? You look like Charles Horsebreaker—his brother, perhaps?"

Distrust struggled with a desire to be worldly in the young Indian. He hated white men, in part because he had been taught to. Another part of him envied them fiercely. He longed to be on easy terms with this lean, steady-eyed rider from Feather Creek. But this was no time for it. He had been warned. . . .

"Go back!" he reiterated menacingly.

Kirk ignored the warning. He well knew what effect a total absence of fear would have on the sentry. Riding close, and hooking a knee over his saddle horn, he forced himself to draw forth tobacco sack and papers, and roll himself a smoke.

"I want a talk with Straight Tongue. He is down

there—isn't he?" He pointed in the direction of the fort.

The guard stared without a movement, without a sign. He was weighing Kirk narrowly.

"Straight Tongue is my friend," Kirk proceeded. "He has done things for me, and I for him. . . . Go down there. Tell him his friend Kirk Jordan wants to see him. I will wait here."

Still the brave did not move. Kirk refrained from glaring at him with the burning impatience he felt. It would take little to turn this fellow sullenly stubborn.

Silence stretched out between them. Flat refusal hovered on the Indian's lips. Even as he opened his mouth to speak the words, Kirk casually handed him the tobacco sack and papers. The brave hesitated.

And hesitating, was lost. Even while his thoughts turned the matter over, his fingers were busy. Never before had a white man—one whom his tribe trusted—asked him to smoke with him. He knew how it was done, however. He went through the gestures of rolling a cigarette and receiving a light with stolid coolness. The action invested him with an importance he would have found it hard to explain.

Kirk let him have his smoke. No words passed. None were needed. Finished, the brave tossed the stub away in the approved fashion. He turned away, his words curt.

175

"I will not be long."

Kirk breathed a great sigh of relief. He had been afraid the deep fears nagging at his spirit would prevent him from using the delicacy of touch required with these fierce-souled, sensitive people. He had won so-far. But another and more rigorous test waited.

The Apache was gone all of half-an-hour. He returned sullen, shooting resentful looks at Kirk now, as if aware that he had been betrayed. However, Straight Tongue was with him.

The latter came directly to Kirk's stirrup. "How you know to come here?" he demanded suspiciously.

Something leaped within Kirk at that. It was virtually a tacit admission that he had not been wrong; that even now Joan might be within no great distance of him. He guarded his tone.

"I wanted to see you, Straight Tongue. I asked Gowan. He put me off, but I insisted. Finally he said I might find you here."

The Apache digested this in silence, looking down. Finally his obsidian eyes raised.

"What you want with me?"

"I am looking for the brown-haired woman," Kirk told him evenly. "She means much to me. I must find her."

Straight Tongue's quick glance was startled. "She is not here!" he declared roughly.

Kirk's voice was as even as ever. "I did not say

176

she was here. I only think you can tell me where she is, Straight Tongue. You have done things for me in the past. Will you do this for me?"

The Apache struggled with himself without any visible signs of it. But Kirk read the pause accurately.

"She is not here," the red lips reiterated doggedly.

Kirk studied the Indian. "I do not ask you to betray your brothers," he said at length, shrewdly. "Take me to your camp."

Straight Tongue rolled this over. His decision was characteristic of him. Without speaking, he turned and started away, tossing over his shoulder at the young brave:

"Watch!"

Kirk followed him. The Apache went rapidly; Kirk never got over his wonder at the speed of these Indians on foot. Ten minutes brought the rakish ruins of old Fort Rader in sight.

The Apaches there made no attempt to hide. Neither did they conceal the instant hostility they felt for this nervy white man. Nearly a dozen of them glared, gathered in a group.

Kirk well knew the potential danger he ran. These savages, every one of them, were bad hombres. They knew they were outside the pale, and that the law had crimes chalked up against them for which they would pay dearly if they were caught. They had no fears of being surprised in this mountain fastness. It was why they were here. Nor was it likely they would withhold their hands if they once decided to do him violence. Only their old trust of him held them in check. Kirk put on a mask of cold stoicism.

One of the Indians spoke gutturally to Straight Tongue. He replied in kind. The exchange was curt, but there was no bickering. Finally Straight Tongue turned to Kirk.

"I have told them what you ask."

"And the answer?"

"We know nothing of the brown-haired one."

Kirk considered. He had no slightest doubt that Joan was here. It was the hardest task he had ever performed to keep his gaze from darting about in search of her.

He said: "I know you have gone on the war path. Your hearts are bad. I say nothing of that. But the Brown-Haired Woman has done nothing. Why should she pay for the mistakes of a grey-haired man?"

Straight Tongue replied that he did not understand. It meant, Kirk understood, that he was not convinced. He summoned all his patience to carry the argument to its fullest. Many words passed. These were conveyed to the hard-faced Apaches, who absorbed them without a sign.

But it became plain that they had nothing against Kirk himself—except that he should not have come here. That was what they didn't like.

It seemed a few of them argued that they should no longer remain here; that they must strike for the rocky peaks, where no white man could possibly follow for any reason.

Kirk held grimly to what fortitude he could muster. He knew these people. It was this very understanding that preserved his life even now.

As though his quest had been settled, Straight Tongue observed woodenly that he had not eaten; he should do so at once. Kirk gave over his pony to a young brave, sank on his heels. A waiting game was better than flat failure.

He ate jerked venison and boiled beef. Some ranchman had contributed unawares to that meal. Kirk wondered if it had been Cole Hutchinson.

Others joined him while he ate. Little or nothing was said. Out of the corner of his eye he tried to determine whether food was carried to one of the tumbledown adobes—to which one. Joan would be there somewhere, he guessed. If she was alive still.

If she had already died, it was little wonder the Indians should refuse to admit any knowledge of her. Kirk tried to estimate whether this was the case. It was torture to fight off these thoughts and at the same time attempt a plan for the future.

Finally Straight Tongue rose, stood beside Kirk as if waiting.

"We go now," he grunted, when Kirk looked up.

The latter rose. A dead weight lay at the pit of

his stomach. Folly to have hoped for anything from these savages! It was enough to turn him to ice to think that he might come this close to Joan, only to be turned back. And there was nothing he could do about it. To lift his hand in anger here and now was to sign his own death-warrant as surely as if he committed suicide.

He waited while his pony was brought. Straight Tongue's bronc was brought also.

Swinging up, Kirk deliberately started out in another direction from the one by which he had come.

"This way!" the Apache warned him sharply.

"No." Kirk was cool. "I go another way."

Straight Tongue looked his interrogation.

"I go to hunt for my wife," Kirk said shortly.

The Indian perceptibly stiffened. "Your— squaw?" he echoed, gaze narrowing.

Kirk saw an advantage he had not thought of before. "Of course. Why should I hunt her, otherwise?" His look was steady. "She was on her way to my home, on the stage."

Straight Tongue whirled to an Indian near at hand. Their words were sharp and quick. A ripple of what might have been surprise ran over the camp.

The Apaches were seeing that Joan at least was no longer on the side of the man they hated. She must have broken with Cole Hutchinson to marry Jordan. Yet there was some hitch. It was a moment before Kirk understood what it was. Then it came to him. To produce the girl now would be their tacit confession of having attacked the stage—a confession of murder.

"The brown-haired one is here," said Straight Tongue abruptly.

Kirk nodded calmly. "I want her."

"She is in that place—" The Indian pointed.

His heart bounding, Kirk started for the adobe indicated. Several Indians tried to stop him. He thrust past. There was a babel of wrathy words behind him as his form darkened the door.

He heard a gasp, then Joan was in his arms. "Kirk! I was afraid you'd never come!"

He soothed her gently. "I'm going to take you away, dear." But he had no slightest idea how it was to be accomplished.

Straight Tongue appeared abruptly in the door. The other Apaches crowded around him, arguing heatedly. He paid no attention to them.

"Take the brown-haired one and leave, quick!" he threw at Kirk.

The latter understood. To get away before this question of right and wrong was settled, was their only chance.

He drew Joan toward the open. Several braves attempted roughly to block his way. But he thrust by, careful to meet the eyes of none of them. His pony was near-by. He hurried his wife toward the animal.

An Indian came toward him, crying out loudly. Kirk swung up in a flash, leaned down and circled Joan with an iron-banded arm. At the same time he touched the bronc with his knee. The bronc started quietly. Kirk lifted the girl up before him. He looked neither to right nor left, but his awareness was bent on the Apaches to read their slightest move.

They were deeply agitated. Suddenly they broke off haranguing Straight Tongue. Kirk heard a rush of moccasins. They were starting for their ponies. They meant to stop him!

Bent over, his lips a straight line, he jammed in the spurs suddenly. The pony started with a bound. In a moment he was flashing across the weather-gullied parade ground at a gallop, headed for the cover of the pines. Yells rang out, fierce and unbridled. He knew the Apaches would be pouring after him without delay. And his bronc was carrying double!

19

Kirk had got started away into the north. His taut anxiety and determination communicated itself to the pony, whose hoofs clattered over the rocks as they fled toward cover and safety. It was not many minutes before the mounted Apaches appeared to the rear. They clung like leeches to their lithe, shaggy broncs, riding like demons.

Kirk would have preferred, after the first few minutes of tension, to swing somewhat eastward, to get down out of the high hills. But the Indians fanned out behind him. Any slightest deviation from his course would mean the loss of valuable seconds.

Had he known what was to come, he would have thanked the red gods of chance that he was forced to go as he did. But for the present he could only bite his thin lips, cast sharp glances over his shoulder and press the pony to greater efforts.

"Will they catch us?" Joan queried, searching his face.

"I'm thinking about what they'll do to us if they don't," was the grim response.

It didn't appear to make sense, and the girl said tightly: "Will they shoot?"

"That's what I'm asking myself." He was

dragging his rifle out of the saddle-boot as he spoke. "One thing is certain: they won't get close to us if I can help it!"

"But they let us leave—"

"No. They didn't know what to do, for a moment; and I took advantage of the deadlock. Straight Tongue would be our friend. Those others—" he broke off expressively.

A blood-curdling Indian yell broke out, echoing. Kirk whirled. They were slowly but surely closing in, sure of the result. Suddenly he whipped up his rifle and let drive at the nearest savage. The Apache's flying pony abruptly did a wild cartwheel, throwing his rider.

A series of wrathy whoops greeted the occurrence. There was a rattle of carbines. Dust flew from the trail ahead, and Kirk felt a rough tug at his arm as a slug grazed him. But the Indians dropped back slightly. They knew this white one's accuracy with a weapon; knew that should he concentrate on red riders instead of ponies, more than one of them would not ride back from the chase. Still they hung on.

"They're farther behind!" Joan cried, looking over Kirk's shoulder.

"Doesn't mean a thing! They're sticking exactly where they want to. We're riding double," he explained; "and when our bronc gives out, they'll have us holed up. They won't have to take any risk. They can simply starve us out."

She shivered in his arms. "What will you do, Kirk?"

"Push on," was his grim answer. It told her, for all her trust in him, how far out of his hands this situation had gone.

Kirk was forced to favor the pony, slowing considerably for an occasional slope. He anxiously watched to note whether the raiders would close in. They wanted to, edging forward. Another shot from his rifle discouraged that.

Old Fort Rader lay miles behind, now. But it would be impossible to keep this pace up, cunningly as Kirk conserved the energy of his mount. Moreover, although Eph Gowan's ranch in the desert basin was nearest, he could not hope to reach there before darkness overtook him.

By midafternoon, their pursuers still clung, more determined than ever. Kirk knew his horse could not hold out much longer. He began casting about in search of just the right place to take cover.

A patch of riven rocks atop a small butte he rejected because there was too much buckbrush surrounding it. He thrust on, and as mile after mile dropped behind he began to wish he had not been so hasty of judgment. Nothing else approaching the butte in possibilities presented itself until Kirk found himself riding across a vast sagebrush hollow in the wooded hills.

Immediately, then, his glance sharpened. A

mile ahead, fairly in the open, a small isolated ridge presented not only a rocky outcrop but the protection of a grove of seedling pines. Kirk struck that way, sweeping the range behind to make sure of the position of the Indians. They noted his object. They began to sweep widely ahead on both sides in a desperate attempt to cut him off or turn him.

But the distance was too short. Kirk reached the high ground with a rush, swinging from the saddle even as he pulled the bronc down. Another minute and he was between barrier ledges, flinging slugs which warned the Apaches to sheer off.

"Get that horse on the ground!" he tossed to Joan. "We may need him again bad. We won't have him if those devils drill him!"

"All right—"

The girl's pluck under the circumstances could not fail to impress Kirk. He had made no mistake, asking her to marry him! Swiftly and without difficulty she forced the pony to kneel and then roll on its side in a protected hollow. She seated herself on its neck then, and cast a look in Kirk's direction.

"If there was only a gun for me," she began; "I might be of some help. The Indians took my gun!"

"Look in that upper saddle-pocket," he directed, without turning. "I think you'll find a six-gun."

186

She did. "Fine! But it's empty, Kirk—"

He punched out a number of cartridges from his belt, which he pocketed. Then opening the belt, he tossed it over. "Crawl to the south," he told her; "and be sure you keep plenty of rocks between you and those Apaches! Watch the brush. Some of 'em are dismounted—don't let a one sneak any closer than you can help!"

She did as directed. The Colt in her grasp began to bang at long intervals. Powdersmoke drifted across the rocks. Slowly the sun swung down the western sky.

Kirk watched its progress with considerable anxiety. What would darkness bring?

The Indians besieged the ridge persistently, attempting one ruse or another, all of which failed. They had abandoned their swift circling on the ponies, and were crawling through the sage like reptiles, unseen except for an occasional spurt of powdersmoke at which Kirk or Joan promptly fired in reply. At long intervals a weird war-cry drifted over the sage, but whether these yells were raised by a brave who had been hit they could not tell.

A copper tint appeared in the sky, and Kirk jerked his eyes upward. The afternoon was old; sunset was scarcely an hour away. Gritting his teeth, he began more determinedly to search the brush for the prowling savages there, but without changing the situation any.

Half-an-hour later he suddenly jerked taut, staring into the north. Something dark and moving appeared there, like—like a herd of steers, he would have said. Hope sprang into flame. He fired several shots, rapidly. The Apache answer rang across the lonely evening brush.

To Kirk's ears, at that, came the thrilling thin song of an army bugle. The cavalry! Then that dark blot in the north swept forward swiftly, resolving into a riding column which at the cry of an officer spread out and began to comb the brush thoroughly. The crack of rifles rang out.

Kirk sprang to the top of the ledge and waved his hat in his excitement. Joan joined him, joy at their deliverance suffusing her face.

"Thank God—!" she breathed.

"Or thank the cavalry!" he finished. "Word must have got to Santa Fe in a hurry!"

A mustached officer saw them, swung his pony that way. Kirk climbed down to meet him.

"Looks like we arrived just nicely in time," the lieutenant smiled frankly.

"You did that," Kirk assured him.

There were a few moments of talk while Kirk told what had taken place. The lieutenant had a number of questions to ask. He said finally:

"If there's anything I can do for you I—I—"

"Thanks. We've a horse here. With no need to hurry, we can make it down the hills all right. If the Apaches haven't wiped out my spread—"

"We passed there. They didn't," was the reply.

A moment later the officer turned back to his command. Kirk turned to Joan.

"We can go now."

They mounted his bronc and jogged away into the dusk. Kirk knew a real discomfort as he stared into the shadows. Another half-hour there on that isolated ridge, and the Indians might easily have crawled forward from so many directions that no defense would have been possible. . . .

Joan's courage touched him deeply. She had been a brave spirit through it all. Even now she was quiet. Had her terrors induced her to break down after what she had passed through, now would have been the time. But she only said softly:

"I knew I could count on you, Kirk. I hadn't the slightest idea how you would manage it. But I clung to that—"

"You can always cling to it," he told her fervently.

After an hour of darkness, the moon came up. It silvered the world of the hills with an unearthly beauty.

A long time later they reached the edge of the mountains. Miles of luminous desert spread away below them, softened to a peaceful kindliness. Kirk was aware of the inherent cruelty underlying that silent prospect. Even Joan shuddered

189

slightly, as though at the touch of the night chill.

They rode down the long slopes into Eph Gowan's basin. Long before they reached the old fellow's ranch, vagrant scents wafted to Kirk's nostrils. He tested them carefully.

"Something's burning—" he murmured at last.

"Or has burnt," she corrected.

He assented. After that they said no more until they came close to Gowan's home. Then it was Joan who burst out:

"Why Kirk, it isn't here any longer!"

His tone was grave: "I was afraid of that." ·

"You mean—"

"The Apaches burned him out," he confirmed. "Straight Tongue wouldn't have done it. But once his pack got started, there was no way of stopping them. They were bent on destroying all the whites they were able."

The thought which sprang into Joan's mind then she left unexpressed. But Kirk entertained the same suspicion. He got down from the pony, leaving her mounted. Approaching the still-glowing mass of coals and ashes which had once been a ranch house, he began a systematic search. There was nothing—no still, awful body lying in the yard. It was possible that Gowan himself had escaped.

A breeze had sprung up. It brightened the sparks of the dying fire, and the sand whispered a low murmur.

"It's already covering the remains," said Joan in an awed voice.

Kirk nodded. In a few days the sand would have covered this spot thoroughly. The desert was claiming its own.

"Take me—home," said Joan brokenly.

He knew what she was thinking, and hastened to comfort her: "I don't believe they'd dare attack the Ladder ranch," he said quickly. "It couldn't have been more than a handful that burned Gowan out. The lieutenant said my place was all right. It's a pretty sure thing that goes for your father's spread."

But he lost no time in mounting and, supporting her, heading in the direction of the Hutchinson outfit.

They had gone scarcely half-a-mile when the murmur of human voices drifted to them.

"Sounds like a search-party," Kirk murmured.

Across the moonlit expanse, the others suddenly spotted them. There was a rush of hoofs. A moment later they were confronted by six riders, who pulled up staring.

Buck Hutchinson's rasping voice broke out: "Why, it's Joan herself! Her and that Jordan—!"

Joan saw that her father and four of his punchers were with Buck. She exclaimed: "Father, is everything all right?"

Instead of answering her, Cole Hutchinson pushed to the fore. His severe face was bleak,

191

his mustache doubly white in the moonlight. His flashing black eyes fastened on Kirk.

"Jordan, I heard the 'Paches was on the warpath an' that they knocked off the stage my girl was ridin' on. . . . S'pose you do some explainin'!"

Kirk did not fully understand him.

"I learned the same thing, Hutchinson. I was driving here with a small herd—"

Pushing to the fore, Buck truculently interrupted: "None of your long-winded explanations, Jordan! *You're* the one that's had Joan all the time. We heard she'd been killed, or worse! Them Apaches 've been your friends right along—doin' yore biddin' an' God knows what not! *You* started this mess to get back at us!"

Ferocity welled up in Kirk at the injustice of this. It was no more than was to be expected of Buck; but he saw no reason why he should swallow the other's accusations.

They glared at each other, their hatred and enmity plain. Kirk grated: "If I thought it would teach you anything—"

There was not the thickness of tissue-paper between peace and red battle in that instant. Buck wanted it. Despite his one whipping, he perhaps thought the men at his back would finish Kirk one way or another.

It was only the other's evident willingness that held Kirk warily back. He scented a trap.

Before he had time to speak, Joan burst out.

"Father, will you allow this? Kirk learned, as you did, that the Apaches had captured me. He acted quicker! If it were not for him, I might be dead now—he saved my life! . . . Is this the way he is to be repaid—to be accused, cursed, and set upon?"

Her father's tone was deliberate, inflexible.

"You got to admit, Joan, he knewed jest where to look fer you. Why does he take it on himself to worry 'bout yuh so much? He said himself he was drivin' stock—"

"I'll tell you why, Hutchinson," Kirk thrust in hardly. "It's because she's my wife!"

A shock ran through them. "What—!"

"We were married in Santa Fe," Kirk drove on. "It was my expectation to tell you immediately I got back here—"

Cole was never more commanding, more forbidding, than in that moment. His flashing glance drilled into his daughter.

"Joan, is this true?"

Her voice was taut. "Yes, Father—"

Buck would have burst out in a volcanic wrath; but Cole cut him off sharply. He directed his indignation and scorn at Joan as he would have pointed a gun.

"That settles it! Yo're no longer chick of mine! I wash my hands of you! . . . See that you get yore belongings out of my house pronto! An' I'm warnin' yuh, girl—never return!"

"But, Father—?" she pleaded, anguish twisting her features.

Cole turned his stiff back.

Joan's head bowed and she wept.

20

Six years rolled over the desert country and the hills. They were peaceful, work-filled years. Such guns as flamed during that time were for the most part to bring down venison, to put an end to the depredations of stock-killing wolves, or simply to keep rope stiffened hands in form.

And yet during those years much had happened. The J Bar ranch in the hills was prosperous now. Even as herds had been driven off to market, others were driven to that high range, which covered the whole of the upland basin now.

The crude cabin Kirk and Pecos had run up was no longer the main building. Kirk had erected a large and comfortable home the next summer after his marriage. Barns stood on the flat beside Feather Creek. The corrals were large and many. The original cabin had become a bunkhouse, where four punchers held forth.

True to his unspoken intention, Pecos had become invaluable during all this time. He acted as ranch superintendent. And he was rigidly efficient. Although Kirk insisted that he was a partner, owning half of all the large outfit, Pecos went his own way. He had from the first denied the possession of a head fitted for business; it was Kirk who transacted the ranch dealings.

All papers were in his name, and Pecos never bothered his thoughts about such things. It was the measure of their mutual confidence.

Joan Jordan took pride in her husband's advancement and success. She had developed, physically and mentally, as he had. The keen edge of early youth was rubbed off them both; but they were still in their vigorous prime, finding a zest in the days, an unfailing support in their love.

Joan had never set foot in the lower basin belonging to her father. She had not seen his face since the night he had ordered her out of his home forever. News of the Ladder ranch seldom trickled up the slopes. When an occasional item did reach Kirk's ears through the drawling gossip of a puncher, he had been wont to pass it on to his wife, until he noted that these occasional bits only added to some deep-hidden distress in her. After that he maintained silence, knowing it for the greater kindness.

The red flames of feud between the two ranches seemed to have died out permanently. Kirk believed Cole Hutchinson responsible for this. The old man must have clamped down on Buck's fevered hatred with a rigid grasp; for whatever his sentiments, Buck had not ventured a show of enmity in any form during the lengthening interval.

Kirk heard that Cole was aging. He could

well believe it. Whatever the rancher's outward show of adamant, the loss of his daughter, as completely as though she had died, must have affected him strongly. Cole, he understood, had given up the active management of the Ladder outfit and Buck was carrying the load on his blunt shoulders these days. It was a diminishing load. Savage desert storms during the years had gradually encroached on the range of the lower ranch, until the Ladder was no longer the imposing spread it once had been.

In the meantime Joan, all unknowing, was kept busy at her own tasks; tasks which brought her a happiness not difficult to understand. She had never found occasion to regret her confidence in Kirk. A son had come to bless their union during the first year of their striving for security. Joan could have wanted for nothing more to fill her days.

Dickie Jordan was already of a size to be on hand at every stock operation concerning the J Bar. "Growin' like a weed," the punchers repeatedly remarked to Kirk, and smiled at his frown. For Dickie was not a weed. He gave promise of becoming a sturdy plant such as his father was. His bright face was open and forthright; the curiosity in his snapping brown eyes, keen. Already he had put his baby-streak behind him. When accident conquered him, he cried silently, squeezing the tears out, and wholly neglected the usual plea for sympathy from whatever direction.

For Pecos at least, Dickie was near to perfection. They were often riding together; and it was from "Uncle Pecos" that the boy learned early many of the tricks of the range and the saddle which in later years were to stand him in good stead.

Dickie, be it said, was close to being the real boss of the J Bar. But they were very careful to keep him from becoming aware of the fact.

One evening a puncher rattled and clattered to a stop outside the Ladder ranch house. He flung out of the saddle and banged on the door sharply.

"Buck, fer Gawd's sake—"

The heavy manager of the Ladder outfit appeared at the door, caught by the tone of this.

"What's up, Ragan?" he rasped.

"Bud Fees has been knocked off—"

"Shot?" Buck snapped.

"Plumb through the chest. He was dead as a mackerel when I found him!"

"Where?"

"Up the hills, not far from Jordan's line!"

Buck's visage hardened. "So that's it, huh?" He asked a few more questions, his look craggy. Having learned all he could he glanced at the sky. There was still an hour of light.

"We'll ride up there," he grunted.

Ragan hurried off to get up a horse for him. Presently they set off. No word was spoken on that ride. Even when Buck saw his puncher's sprawled body in the brush, he only drew in his lips and dismounting, began a careful search of the ground.

There was nothing near at hand. Buck remounted and splashed across the creek. Here, in the brush, he found the tracks of a single bronc. He and Ragan followed them a ways, studying.

"Hind hoofs slew in, like that bronc Pecos Johnson rides," the puncher growled.

Buck nodded. "Noticed it . . . It was Johnson, all right!"

It was singularly poor evidence on which he had passed judgment; but he did not pause to consider that. During the years, he had looked up the hills often toward the J Bar spread, hatred and bitter envy twisting his heart. All this time he had watched for the slightest excuse to reopen the feud. Cole Hutchinson had stood in his way at first. It was different now.

His tone was like a file: "Johnson took it on himself to sting us again, that's plain. I dunno why he did it—maybe life is gettin' too dull for him! But there's one thing there ain't any doubt about, damn his rotten hide—and that's what I'm goin' to do about it!"

"Why not ride up there now an' get it over with?" Ragan threw out truculently. "We can cut out Johnson, the two of us, an' settle his hash in a hurry!"

Buck vetoed that. "I'll take care of this, and do it in my own way! . . . Quarter the brush, Ragan, till you find Fees' bronc. Tie him on it and get him down to the ranch."

There was so much finality in this that the puncher did not venture to argue. Buck swung back to his saddle. Hunched there like a block of stone, he headed away without any sign of his intentions, his grim thoughts playing in his brain like lightning.

"Where's Pecos?" Kirk asked one of his punchers, in the J Bar ranch yard the following afternoon. "I haven't laid eyes on him for several hours."

"Dunno, Kirk. Mebbe he's huntin' for his bronc."

The little man's favorite pony had apparently broken pasture a day or so before and had been missing since. Pecos had fumed a bit, riding out to make a survey of the range. He had returned empty-handed but unsatisfied.

"Don't worry about it," Kirk had advised him. "One of the boys'll run across it presently and run it in."

Pecos had had little to say, but evidently he had his own ideas. He had ridden into this country on that bronc. He didn't want to lose it. And so, without a word he was putting on a real hunt for it.

This at any rate was the conclusion Kirk arrived at. He let it go for the time-being. But Pecos did not put in an appearance as he expected him to. The day ended, and still the gnarled little man was among the missing.

"Queer," he frowned. "It isn't like him to stay away like this without saying something—"

"He'll show up when he gets around to it, dear," Joan said over the supper table. "He thinks the world of that bay horse." She laughed. "Probably dusk caught him farther from home than he expected to be. He's probably on his way back now."

"Uncle Pecos promised he'd take me widing up Geronimo tomorrow," Dickie piped, his tousled head just showing above the edge of the table. "He better tum back!"

For once, Kirk could not see the humor in the child's idle prattle.

"I don't like it," he declared. "If he isn't back before bed-time—"

"What, dear?" his wife queried.

Kirk did not answer, but his face was pre-occupied as he finished his meal and moved away from the table. More than once during the evening he made his way out to the bunkhouse. Each time the answer was the same.

Kirk never had been a prey to causeless alarm.

201

But this time some instinct told him to be on his guard. He was up in the morning before dawn. A look in the bunkhouse, where Pecos had always preferred to live, showed him the latter had not returned.

Without waiting for breakfast, Kirk saddled up and set out. The lifting golden segment of the rising sun found him far on the range in the Upper Basin. He rode at a brisk pace, now scanning the distance; now studying the soil underfoot with care.

It was not by accident that he stumbled over Pecos's tracks at length. For he knew the little man so well by now that he could follow his mental processes closely. Pecos, naturally, had been trying to read the vagrant impulses of a straying horse. The pony, he had reasoned, would take a general downward course and its sign would be plain in one of the natural outlets to the lower land.

It was at one such spot that Pecos's own trail appeared. Once he spotted it, Kirk had no doubt. No one but his old partner would have made just this kind of a trail—not direct, but turning this way and that, in obvious search.

Kirk followed it downward. The way led along the descending gorge of Feather Creek, where it worked its way into a lower canyon bastioned with rocky walls. At places Pecos had been forced to sheer away from the broken, rugged boulder patches; at others he had come closer, to ride along the edge of the gaping chasm.

Kirk looked forward constantly now. He was nearing Ladder range. Even so, he was surprised at the sudden clatter of hooves, on rock which sounded from beyond a rocky corner.

He made the turn—and there was a riderless pony, cropping the tufted grass of this little trailside recess; scrambling up the rubble along the walls to snatch daintily at the highest tufts. But what arrested Kirk was the fact that it bore its bridle still, the lines dragging; and on its back was cinched an old saddle belonging to Pecos.

Kirk swung down to the ground, his face blanching. On the range, he would have thought nothing of Pecos afoot; but there on the edge of this gorge—

"Something's happened to him!" he jerked out.

A study of the trail gave him no immediate clue. Whether his partner had been thrown, to lay somewhere nearby with a broken leg; or whether the bronc had given him the slip while he had a look around, was not clear. Making his way to the canyon's edge, he looked over into the depths.

Space opened out down there, fanged with rocks. Suddenly his breath stopped. On a ledge a hundred feet below lay a crumpled figure. Kirk didn't need the familiar clothing, the rumpled head of rust-colored hair, to tell him who it was.

Pecos had come to the end of his trail. Of that

Kirk was somehow sure, even before he crawled down and reached the perilous ledge. When he arrived, however, another shock awaited him. Pecos had been murdered! The shot had ranged upward through the back of his head and come out at the line of the forehead.

Rage gripped Kirk and shook him fiercely. That any man should have taken his partner's life so ruthlessly seemed to him incredible. Kneeling there over the still form, he lifted his gaze, looking bitterly down the canyon. He found himself seeing, beyond the canyon's mouth, the tumbled acres of the Ladder range.

A thought struck him. Buck Hutchinson! Could he have done this? Into Kirk's mind flashed memory of things Pecos had told him from time to time—of meetings with Buck at Beartrack, and Buck's truculent desire for trouble. The matter had grown worse, until Pecos had been forced to lash Buck with a coiled rope. Nor had it stopped there. It had gone on—to this.

Struggling back up the broken cliff to the trail, Kirk was sure he had the answer. He was not long in reaching certain conclusions of his own. Only one move remained for him: He must get Buck before Buck got him. Once the latter had started his bloody work, he would know better than to stop before his work was done. Kirk had not much time to spare.

But first there was Pecos to be gotten back

to the J Bar. Kirk fastened him across his own saddle, and mounting his own bronc, started out.

He had scarcely gotten off the canyon trail before sudden sounds from ahead broke in upon his dour abstraction. He snapped taut in a flash. The trail led up and down through scattered pines. Pulling up, he rode off the trail and stopped in a concealing grove. He snaked his rifle out of the boot as he slipped to the ground. Then he was moving forward on foot.

For a time all was silent. Then he heard the sound again—the incautious rasp of a horseshoe on rock. A hundred yards ahead a chipmunk came scooting around a gnarled trunk and turned to look back, its tail twitching angrily.

Kirk worked forward, keeping under cover. He scarcely knew what to expect, but it was in his mind that he would suddenly meet Buck Hutchinson. It was like the man to want to close accounts in short order.

"We'll see what he's got to say!" Kirk gritted.

He wormed on cautiously, his rifle at the ready. Now through a screen of scrub he spotted a plaid-covered shoulder, the brim of a hat. Whoever it was, was afoot, leading his mount. The blood heated Kirk. "Laying for me too!" was his thought.

Suddenly he broke cover, the gun-muzzle thrust out.

"Up with 'em!"

To his amazement, it was not Buck Hutchinson who whirled on his heels, to stare transfixed. It was Eph Gowan! Gowan, whom for six years he had thought dead. Gowan, who hated Cole Hutchinson with an undying hatred!

The amazement was mutual. It was for this reason that for a long moment no word was spoken as they exchanged bleak stares. And during that moment a flash of insight visited Kirk. Eph Gowan's chagrin at having been discovered was patent. And that explained everything.

Gowan was responsible for Pecos's murder! Out of some impulse of his twisted brain, he had returned after these years with the hope of reviving the old feud; still hoping to smash Cole Hutchinson for some injury of the past; but now more cunning, ruthless and demented than ever. It sent a chill of disquiet shuddering over the young man, as though he stood on the edge of an abyss of horror.

21

"You better put that gun down!" Gowan blurted suddenly. A flush of blood mounted to his veined and age-carved face. He had aged far more than six years would have warranted, Kirk saw. There was something vital gone out of him, as though stalwart manhood had shriveled. In its place was coiled something covert and crafty that was like a warning.

Kirk lowered the rifle barrel, but not so far that he could not bring it up sharply at need.

"What are you doing here?" he snapped.

"Hell of a note if a man can't travel what was once his own range without answerin' a pile of fool questions!" Old Eph retorted waspishly. He seemed watching the effect of his words on Kirk. His eyes dilated. "Why shouldn't I come back here? Who's got a better right?"

Kirk's dry skepticism was noncommittal. "How long have you been around?"

Gowan made a violent gesture. "There yuh go, treatin' me like a danged lawyer!" He shoved his jaw forward. "Wasn't it me, put yuh where yuh are now? Wasn't it, huh? . . . While yo're so damn anxious to chase me away, why haven't yuh seen to it yuh run Cole Hutchinson often this range?"

Kirk considered this last an adequate answer

to his last question. Evidently Eph had been around long enough to have found out that Cole's Ladder brand still ran cows on this range. Seeing the Ladder steers would not have been enough; for that way there would be no way of knowing whether Hutchinson had sold out to someone else.

Mention of his ancient enemy appeared to increase Gowan's blood pressure. He appeared to swell in the face, and his lips trembled.

"Never mind! There's a better One than you fightin' on my side! The One Who made all this—He's seein' to Cole Hutchinson, slow an' shore, so's he'll feel every turn of the screw!" Words tumbled from Old Eph's mouth in gushing profusion. "Damn him, I'll go down there an' laugh in his face! The desert's drivin' him out—it don't take nothin' else to do it; an' it won't be long, either! He ain't got a quarter of the grass he had six years ago!" And he laughed wickedly.

Kirk fell back a step. The action was involuntary. There was almost a note of madness in Gowan's hysterical intensity. His hatred of Cole Hutchinson had not cooled to dead ashes. It had grown till it was a taut bow-string in him. It had become the mainspring of his existence.

"He's twisted outa my hands a dozen times, like the crawlin' snake he is!" he babbled on, fiercely. "He can't worm away this time! I ain't gone so far that I don't know what's been goin' on in this country. Ever' time they was a sandstorm here I knowed about it; just the same as if I was here, I seen the sky git red an' the sand come creepin' an' crawlin' in—smotherin' Cole Hutchinson as shore as if 'twas hands on his gullet!"

On and on the impassioned words flowed. Gowan seemed to lose control of himself as he continued. Veins in his eyes reddened; his hands flashed like clawed things, his body writhed. He was working himself up to a pitch which no man could withstand. Kirk was on the point of interceding, even if it came to the use of force, when Gowan suddenly broke off, his visage a ghastly purple. He gasped and staggered, pawing at his throat. Then before Kirk's hands could reach him, he slumped to the ground.

Pity threaded Kirk's hot impatience. He suspected Gowan's brain had been near the cracking point. Perhaps this faint had saved his reason. Bringing him out of it would only drag him back to his torment, but there seemed nothing else to be done.

Yet all Kirk could do failed of its effect. Breathing stertorously, Old Eph lay as though otherwise dead. Kirk gave up presently.

"Have to get him back to the spread," he murmured. "Can't leave him here, that's certain."

He bolstered Gowan across his saddle and fastened him there. Then he led back to where his own bronc waited. Pecos, stretched over his own saddle, brought a groan from Kirk.

"Pecos didn't deserve this," he told himself. "It goes to show what hate does. It hits at everybody within striking distance!"

His arrival at the J Bar, an hour later, created considerable excitement. He reached the bunkhouse in such a way that Joan would not be subjected to the grisly sight of the two grimly laden broncs, and got both Pecos and Gowan attended to. The cook helped him, clucking his tongue.

For Pecos there was nothing to be done but arrange his funeral. Joan had to be told what had happened. She took it hardly, for she had held great respect for the gnarled little man. Whatever her opinion of Eph Gowan was, she did not state it.

"If Gowan killed Pecos—and I'm practically certain he did," Kirk told her, "he is scarcely responsible. It was his crack-brained way of attempting to start up the feud again." To himself, he added: "And he blame near did it!"

Dickie was disconsolate. He had loved his Uncle Pecos in an inarticulate way; the latter's death was the first real blow he had ever received from life. He had to be told that Pecos's bronc had thrown him to his fate; but that harmless deception did little to soften his grief.

Range men from far and near came to the funeral. Pecos had made an astonishing number of friends. Meanwhile, Eph Gowan had regained consciousness and was among those present. If it impressed him that this was the burial of his own victim, he made no sign that it affected him. He seemed absent-minded, mumbling to himself; he paid little attention to what went on around him.

This state continued afterward. Kirk scarcely knew what to do with the old fellow. He couldn't turn him off to die of neglect on the range. Gowan appeared capable of answering only the most simple questions. Any inquiry as to his present home, or as to what he wanted to do, met with a blank wall of uncomprehending silence.

Kirk shrugged when asked what was to be done. While there was a potential threat in Old Eph's presence, he seemed to have lost his memory. Perhaps from now on he would be harmless.

"Let him do odd jobs," Kirk grunted. "He may come out of it, and he may not—"

So Gowan, a shambling, slow figure now, fitted into the life of the J Bar and gradually sank back out of the notice of most. But Kirk, thinking grimly of Pecos, could not forget. His feelings were mixed every time his eyes fell on the old fellow, and it was not from preference that he let Gowan stay on the ranch.

Dickie was told to stay away from Old Eph. The boy failed to connect Gowan in his mind with his Uncle Pecos's fate, of course; he had rather an interest in the bearded, slow shuffling old man. But Kirk made him understand that Eph was to be let alone.

"He's not well," he told his son. "He wants to be left to himself. Now, don't make me tell you this again. . . ."

His eyes large as he listened, Dickie was only filled with a large curiosity as well. He would have cultivated Old Eph in his own way, but that he had an enormous respect for the commands of his father. Besides which, he was at an age when there was a world of wonders beckoning. Not even the memory of Uncle Pecos could make him sad for long.

He was rapidly making friends with the world of experience. Gone were the days when he must watch without doing. Kirk had given him a small, shaggy-haired and long-legged pony and a saddle to match. In a week's time he had mastered the art of saddling; and to remain on a horse was with him a matter of instinct.

He rode over the range in the Upper Basin until he knew its acres almost as well as the punchers. His mind was busy too. His mother had begun to tell him "growed-up things," and he turned these over in the thorough, inquisitive way of a child.

He knew, for instance, that down under the hills lived a grandfather whose face he had never seen. It did not strike him as particularly strange, but there were times when he considered the exciting notion of doing something about it. What did a grandfather look like? His mother had tried to tell him—not like Daddy, not like Pecos, nor like Old Eph either. From her descriptions the boy drew a picture of a stern old man whose glance was like that of an eagle and whose voice might have belonged to a bear. All this failed to deter his desire to know more.

He knew where his grandfather lived, too. More than once his mother had pointed out the way. At last he had teased her to go down there— "Just you and me, Mommy. Please!"

But she shook her head, refusing after the mysterious manner of parents. "No, Dickie. I mustn't go. And you mustn't." She tried to impress this on him.

"Haven't you never beened down there?" he queried.

Her smile was sad—or maybe that was a shadow on her face, which he knew so well. "Yes. A long time ago, Dickie. . . . Run along, now, and don't ask so many questions."

So Dickie got no more information that time. The only time he had ever mentioned his grandfather to his father, the latter scowled swiftly.

"What are you talking about, son? Who told you you had a grandfather down by the desert?"

Dickie knew at once that he'd made a mistake. "Well—Mother told me!"

It seemed to cut off whatever his father was

about to say. But the boy understood. His grandfather was a subject on which his father did not care to speak.

All these things only added the seasoning of mystery to the child's speculations. More and more he wanted to penetrate the secret of his grandfather for himself.

Therefore it was in the nature of an exploration when, one afternoon, without saying a word to anyone he saddled up and set off down the hills. It was rough going for the pony, but Dickie did not mind. He had patience.

He had never been so far from home when at last he saw the Ladder ranch a long ways below him. Sure now that this was his objective, he yet hesitated. Should he go so far? He knew he was doing wrong. But curiosity was like a spur rowel behind his impulses, thrusting him on.

Half-an-hour later he rode into the sandy ranch yard. There was a huge pepper tree opposite the gallery. Its leaves looked as if they were dying. All else that had once been green had long since died in this spot.

Before the gallery a saddled horse dozed, hip-slanted. On the gallery itself an old man sat in a rawhided chair, one leg across his other knee, his hands folded, motionless. Dickie became alert. Was that his grandfather?

A door at the end of the house slammed and a husky man came through. He started for the waiting saddle-horse, then seeing Dickie's approach, caused to scowl.

After the first searching scrutiny, Buck Hutchinson instinctively knew who this was. Kirk Jordan's kid! A gust of wrath shook him and his visage darkened.

"What you doin' down here?" he demanded roughly.

Dickie drew in to gaze at him surprised. He piped: "I'm looking for my Drandfather."

"He ain't here. Go on home!" Buck would have sounded even more fierce had he dared to raise his voice. No telling where the old man was right now—

The boy was crestfallen. "You mean—Dickie tan't stay?"

"That's what I mean! Git that pony turned around and—"

"Shut up, Buck!" The harsh command of Cole Hutchinson came clear and cutting from the gallery. "Go on away yoreself, and mind yore own business!"

Buck started in surprise, then flushed with a fresh access of anger.

"Why, dammit all—"

"You heard me!" Cole bellowed.

Buck's head jerked up. With a curled lip, he strode to his bronc, swung aboard and jogged away, glaring at the boy as though he could kill him.

Dickie understood that in some way Buck's orders were nullified.

He kneed the tired pony ahead toward the gallery. The old man was still sitting there where he had been. For a long, thoughtful moment the young boy and the man exchanged looks.

"Are you my Drandfather, man?" Dickie asked.

"I don' know. That's accordin' to who yuh are," Cole replied with intentional gruffness. Something was happening within him—something he had never expected; and he was trying mightily to guard against it.

"I'm Dickie Jordan!"

Cole contented himself with staring at him, his face a wooden mask. So this was Joan's child! And Kirk Jordan——he too, stuck out all over the boy, in his cool, deliberate regard, his well-chiseled chin.

"You *are* my Drandfather, aren't you?" Dickie persisted.

"Mebbe I am," Cole responded uneasily.

Dickie slid down and came slowly to the edge of the gallery. He displayed impatience.

"Either you are or you aren't, man!"

It was too much for Cole. Involuntarily he grinned. "Wal then we'll say I am," he conceded.

Dickie nodded with engaging simplicity. "That's better. My mother didn't tell me you look just like what you do—but you know how women are. Daddy says they're nice, but you have to keep an eye on 'em. . . . Drandfather, when you keep an eye on anything, how can you go 'way and leave it?"

It did not take much of this brand of attack to reduce Cole completely. Whatever his reservations against this child, he gave over without a struggle.

They had a fine afternoon, the two of them, once the hard-bitten rancher gave in at last. He knew now that this was exactly what he had wanted, what he had craved deep within him from the moment he learned, long ago now, that Joan had a son. He had told himself he wanted to see the boy, from a distance if no more. And now that he had not only seen him but got to know a little the child's charm of character, he would have given more than he would ever admit to tear down the wall he had himself built between himself and his daughter.

But he put this away from him quickly, jealous of the passing minutes. He wanted all of this grandchild he could claim; and it was just possible that once they learned in the Upper Basin where Dickie had been, they would never let him come again.

For this same reason it was late when Cole gave up to the knowledge that he must let the boy go for today. He had a bronc saddled up for himself, and rode with the youngster some ways up into the hills, to make sure he did not lose his way.

217

The sun dropped lower, until it was hidden behind the shoulder of Geronimo. Cole drew rein.

"Wal—so long, tike," he said gruffly.

"You won't tome any farther, Drandfather?"

"No—" Cole fumbled his reins a moment. "Come see me again if you can," he added, in a muffled tone.

"Of course I will, Drandfather."

So they parted, the boy proceeding up the slope with many a backward glance; the old man riding downward, heavily, the weight of all his years resting on him.

22

Dusk was sifting down over the range when Kirk slammed into the house from his work. An unusual silence struck him at once.

"Where's Dick?" he called.

Coming through from the kitchen, Joan glanced at him slowly as her attention was caught.

"Why, wasn't he out at the corrals?"

"No—"

They exchanged thoughtful looks.

"Kirk, he hasn't been in the house all afternoon. I felt sure he was with you!"

Kirk hid the small shock of surprise the words gave him. He half-turned away.

"He must be on some excursion of his own. I'll see if I can't scare him up. . . ."

"But, dear!" Joan was not to be put off thus. "You would have seen him if he had been anywhere around the ranch yard!"

"Not if I was busy," he grunted. Even as he turned toward the door his mind was busy with the problem. What had become of the boy? It was Dickie's privilege to ride where he pleased in the Upper Basin. He often did so. But seldom was it that he failed to put in an appearance a full hour before dark.

Kirk thrust away the thought that wormed

its insidious suggestion through the back of his mind. He didn't want to face it. But he knew at bottom that he must do so sooner or later. Suppose Buck Hutchinson had Dickie?

He frowned over that as, moving about the yard, his eye ran here and there without catching sight of the small figure of his son. He heard the kitchen screen slam as Joan followed him out, to scan the dusk-mantled range anxiously.

Buff Cleghorn, Kirk's foreman, came moving up from the work corrals. He headed for the saddle-shed. Kirk called to him:

"Was the boy with the horses when you came away, Buff?"

Cleghorn paused to stare. Then without answering immediately he moved toward Kirk.

"Why, no, Kirk. What's the trouble—the little devil turn up missin'?"

"Can't seem to lay hands on him." Kirk was still calm about it. But now Joan moved forward. There was a catch in her voice.

"You had better look for him, Kirk. I don't like his being away after dark!"

"It isn't dark yet—"

It was so obvious an attempt to reassure that she didn't even reply to it.

Buff said: "I'll get up a bronc for yuh, Kirk." He turned hurriedly away.

He came back in a few moments leading two mounts. Kirk and Joan had discussed the situation meanwhile. Dickie's mother was even more worried than before.

"Let me have the other pony, Buff," she said tautly. "I'm going to hunt too!"

Cleghorn expostulated mildly. There was no need for worry. He was sure of it. The boy had simply got farther away from home than he expected, and sunset had overtaken him. "He'll be along in no time, never fear."

Joan said: "Yes—" But she did not relinquish her intention, taking the bridle and swinging up. Kirk had already started to ride away. She followed him.

They met a puncher returning across the range, not far from the ranch. Kirk's tone was clipped and direct now:

"Seen Dickie, Red?"

"Wal—" said Red, and provokingly broke off. "Seems I did see him some'eres. . . . Nigh on two o'clock, it was. He was up on that half-pint bronc of his—"

"Where was he going?" Kirk snapped.

"Wal—he was headin' down the basin when I seen 'im."

Kirk said no more, wheeling away. His wife was still at his heels. Red stared after them, and then burst out:

"Hey! Yuh ain't tellin' me he's lost?"

"Don't know," Kirk threw over his shoulder, without stopping.

The puncher grunted "huh!" his face serious, and altering his original direction, started away on a hunt of his own.

Kirk and Joan rode for some minutes in silence. It was the latter who spoke, finally.

"Kirk, you don't think anything could have— happened to him, down this way?"

He knew by this that she entertained the same distrust of Buck Hutchinson as himself. His response was curt:

"If he was going to get thrown off his bronc, it might happen to him anywhere."

Her breath sucked in at that. Even so, it seemed a more merciful thing than that other—

This darkness was enough to make one think all sorts of lurid thoughts. Of one thing she was sure: that Dickie would not remain away from home, in the night, for any reason except that he was unable to get there.

Later an early moon flashed over the hills to spill silver down the slopes. They had searched long; hope was at low ebb. It was Kirk who suddenly jammed in the spurs and jumped his horse forward toward a moving black blot.

"Daddy! Is that you?" came the untroubled, treble query.

It sent a stab of relief through the parents. Kirk, at least, was left with a reaction of severity.

"Where've you been, young man?"

"Down there." The boy swung an arm down

the slope behind him. "I went down to see my Drandfather!"

Blank silence.

"And did you—see him?" Dickie's mother inquired, faintly.

"Why, of tourse!" The boy's surprise was innocent.

Kirk's jaws set with instinctive opposition. "Are you aware you've given your mother and father a good scare?" he demanded. "I don't want this to happen again! Understand me—you're not to go down there again, ever!"

It was largely on Joan's account that he spoke thus. But the boy failed to understand. Tears welled in his eyes, rolled down his cheeks silently.

"Then tan't I see my Drandfather no more?" he asked with direct simplicity.

Kirk understood that Cole Hutchinson must have kept the boy down there, whether deliberately or not; until he should have to start back so late. For that if for nothing else, Cole earned his quick resentment. His glance caught at something. His big hand reached out.

"What is that?" he demanded.

He could see what it was: a braided leather quirt which he had never seen in his son's possession before. But he did not mean his question literally. Even as he looked closely at the thing, it came to him. It was a gift to the boy from his grandfather—a peace offering or a bribe.

In the act of tossing it away into the brush with an angry snort, Kirk paused. His glance fell on his wife's face. There was a look there he had not seen before. Was it the effect of the moonlight? Joan looked undeniably wistful, sad—

"What you going to do with my quirt, Daddy?" Dickie demanded. "Dive it back to me!"

Plainly enough, his desire for the thing was keen. Even Joan made an involuntary gesture, as if to reach for it and give it to him.

Of a sudden, without bidding, it came over Kirk like a change of heart: Why go on with this hatred and enmity? He had nothing, personally, against Cole Hutchinson. It had been wholly at the will of the old man himself that a barrier lay between the two ranches. Clearly the way lay open, in this child, for a reconciliation. Kirk knew only too well what it would mean to Joan, who from the start had been innocent of blame, yet on whom most of the feud's weight had fallen.

He said nothing then. Such a change in his thinking required a twist in the fixed attitude of six years' living. But his action was enough and more than enough to reveal to Joan what he felt. Without a further word, he handed the braided quirt back to his son.

"Well . . . we'd better be getting back to the ranch if we're going to have any supper tonight," he remarked gruffly.

Even the boy realized that some crisis had been safely passed. He became all smiles again, and presently was jogging jauntily along ahead of his parents.

They watched him with unaccountable warmth stirring in their hearts.

When Buck Hutchinson pulled himself astride his pony and rode away from the Ladder ranch house that afternoon, he had not gone, indifferent, to his work as Cole supposed he had. Once out of sight beyond a rocky knoll, Buck pulled up, got down and turned back toward the house. Later he crouched and crawled to a rock from which he had an unobstructed view of the shady gallery.

For a long time he sat on his heels, his gaze unwavering. Finally he reached up and pulled off his hat like a man presented with a problem. The fingers scratching through his stiff, bristly hair seemed to help him none at all.

"Somethin's got to be done about this," he growled to himself, his face speculative and cruel.

He was not for an instant deceived by the apparently innocent look of Kirk Jordan's boy coming down to visit Cole Hutchinson—and Cole, after some undecided sparring, giving him welcome.

To Buck's mind, overheated by ready hatred and suspicion, it threatened the downfall of all he hoped for. His patience, he prided himself, had been long indeed. For six years he had bided his time.

While he had raved and cursed against Kirk at the time, he had been glad enough to see Joan go with the other. It could not have been arranged better for him, to have Cole cast his daughter off forever. With Buck the only one who remained, the Ladder brand must fall into his hands when Cole passed on.

It wasn't much in these days, the Ladder—a huge ranch, true, but sadly fallen away from what it once had been. Buck had watched the storms encroach steadily, like the advance of fate, and had said nothing. Actually it mattered little enough to him. He had another object in view.

Once he was in undisputed possession of the Ladder, with Cole safely beyond the grave, he meant to launch an attack against Kirk Jordan which the other would find it impossible to withstand. In a short time, Buck promised himself, Jordan would be forced to abandon the Upper Basin. Then Buck would move up there with the Ladder herds; build himself a reputation and a stronghold in the hills which would be impregnable.

It was this dream that the arrival of Dickie Jordan threatened. Of course, it might be that Buck overestimated the seriousness of affairs.

The boy might never come again. . . . He shook his bullet head at that.

"By God, I don't dare leave it to chance!" he swore in a harsh undertone.

But what was he to do? Settling himself farther behind the rock, he rolled a smoke and sucked it while he turned things over in his mind. Every wolfish instinct in him warned him that this was no time for making a snap decision. He must settle accounts once for all.

"I could watch when the kid heads for home," he thought; "grab him and knock him off—or take him away somewheres. . . ."

He sat thinking about that. Crows-feet appeared at the corners of his eyes with the intensity of his effort, and sweat gently rolled down his temples.

"If the kid's found dead on Ladder range, that'd turn Jordan and his wife dead against the old man for good and all, that's certain. . . . But Cole wouldn't stand for it. He'd remember I seen the kid at the house and tried to send him back. The old devil'd throw it up to my face!"

He could stand that, he knew. But if he held his ground, what would Cole do then? He might spread the news of his suspicion; there'd be an official investigation, all kinds of a mess stirred up. No—Buck couldn't have that. Cole might even turn him off cold, throw him off the spread.

"No, I don't dare lay a finger on the kid."

It angered him deeply because it was so final.

227

There was no open trail that way. Then what— knock off Cole himself, in some way that would look natural? No—Jordan! *It was Kirk Jordan who must be got out of the way!*

Buck's jaws clamped as he arrived at this point. He knew he had reached the inevitable end of his thinking; that his course lay open before him, with no other way to turn.

He was satisfied. "It's Jordan or me," he grated. "That's what it would be as long as the two of us last. . . . I'll get him before he gets me!"

But he could not move at once. He determined with inhuman craft that not by so much as a breath would Jordan's finish ever be laid to him. He decided to wait two or three days, so that not even Cole would think to connect up a sudden slaying on the range with the visit of Jordan's boy to the Ladder spread.

It was hard waiting. Now that he had made up his mind, Buck never did anything that made more of a demand on him than simply allowing time to pass between decision and accomplishment.

On the second evening he set out, making sure that no one saw him taking leave of the Ladder. His rifle bulked in its boot under his leg; there was jerky in his slicker-roll, for he knew it might take considerable time. Still he did not hurry.

His way took him to Beartrack, where he further fed the fires of hatred with much raw spirit. Then casually dropping the remark that he meant to ride north for a couple of days, looking at horses, he left the canyon crossing in early morning.

Climbing the hills then, he bedded down for a couple of hours in a place no one could possibly have found. With the sun's rise, he rose and pushed on.

Midmorning brought him close to the J Bar spread. From a height he studied the Upper Basin for over an hour, making doubly sure that he was familiar with its every corner. Then he pushed on down the slopes. He had seen someone ride away from the Jordan ranch, and now he proceeded with his rifle across his knees.

From a lower ridge he had another look, and this time he made out his man, much closer. He was sure it was Kirk: His muscles snapped taut. He made sure of exactly where Kirk was heading—then throwing in the spurs, he headed across a short-cut to intercept the other.

Ten minutes later he slacked his pace. A rocky ridge seemed to divide him from his enemy's course. He slid out of the saddle. His blood was like ice now. With the stealth of a mountain lion, he stole up a gully toward the ledge above.

Reaching there, it was as though his breath were shut off. He peered out and down, cautiously. Of a sudden a thrill coursed over him; a flash of savage exultation. There was his enemy, riding all unconscious of peril. In another moment he would come within a hundred yards. Buck's clawlike hands tightened on his gun.

23

Although Kirk had not, there was another man in the basin who had seen Buck. For all his absent-mindedness Eph Gowan had lost none of his keenness of eye. He had spotted Buck high in the hills on his first entering the basin, like a vulture perched on its vantage point.

Though he had been disarmed on arrival at the J Bar, weeks ago now, Gowan with senile cunning had managed to unearth an old six-shooter which he carried concealed on his person. Exactly why, he could not have said; but the sight of Buck Hutchinson, whom he observed skulking down the hills, brought enough of his old life back to put him on the alert.

He traced Buck's stealthy movements for some time. Later he observed Kirk leaving the ranch on his usual business, and noted that Buck sought to put himself in the other's trail. Old Eph read what was afoot. His hackles rose. Snatching out his gun, he pushed his bronc forward, unseen by either the stalked or the stalker.

He reached the ridge atop which Buck lay ambushed. Without a sound he slid out of the saddle and began creeping through the brush. His face looked carved out of red rock now, and there was something predatory in it. His white brows gave his eyes an indescribably fierce look.

He made his way from one boulder to another like a wolf, for he was near Buck's hiding-place. Chaotic impressions swirled in his warped brain. He entertained no doubt that this man was his deadly foe, instinct assuring him of what intelligence could not.

Buck was all unconscious of this menace creeping toward him along the ridge. His ears were cocked for the faint hoof-clicks of Kirk's bronc. His rifle hovered, ready to flame.

Suddenly there was the faintest kind of a sound, coming from the rocks on Buck's left. He tossed an impatient glance that way—and froze, his jaw dropping. For a split-second amazement made him incapable of movement.

He recognized Eph Gowan in a flash. The old man crouched in a gap between two rocks, his visage twisted with hatred, a six-gun in his clawlike hand. How he had got there Buck hadn't the slightest notion. He could not have been more surprised had he seen a ghost.

But he was in the prime of life, his reflexes keen. Only for that single fleeting instant did he remain helpless. Even as Gowan threw up the six-gun with a soundless snarl, Buck swept the rifle barrel toward him.

Roaring gunfire split the quiet. Buck felt the cold flutter of a slug past his face. He fired from the hip, but there was nothing random about his aim. His own bullet tore out Gowan's throat and made the old man stagger.

It was so swift that Old Eph never knew what struck him. No astonishment visited his features. His eyes went blank, like suddenly turned-out lamps. He swayed—tumbled forward in an ungainly sprawl.

"Gawd! That was close!" Buck grunted through clenched teeth.

The question passed through his mind in a flash whether he could finish Kirk Jordan also at this one stroke. He threw a hasty glance over the ledge. Kirk was not in sight, but a crashing amidst the trees told him the other was not far off—probably dashing this way furiously, to learn the cause of this gunfire on his own range.

Moisture sprang out on Buck's forehead. He had no remote chance of taking Kirk by surprise now. There remained the opening for an out-and-out duel, if he wanted to shoot it out with the other. Neither would enjoy any notable advantage; the outcome resting on the lap of the gods.

Buck weighed the thing and made his decision in a second's time. Wheeling, he burst running from the spot in a mad attempt to reach his bronc and steal away before Kirk could learn his identity. There was always the chance, he told himself, to come back and do this job right.

He succeeded in reaching his horse, flung

himself into the hull and jammed home the spurs. Then he was flashing through the trees on a dead run.

Topping the ridge, Kirk caught the sound of his going, already distant. Pushing his bronc, he flashed by the spot where Buck had waited to ambush him. Something caught his eye— Gowan's crumpled form, there in the rocks. Involuntarily Kirk drew in. His face was bleak. Murder had been done here!

He looked the way the assassin had gone, his eyes hard. The faint sounds of a horse had already died away. "I'll take care of you in good time!" Kirk thought, and turned back to dismount beside Eph Gowan.

He could scarcely repress an exclamation when he saw who it was. He noted the gun which had dropped from Eph's loosening fingers.

"I often wondered if you were playing dumb, old man," he mused. "It seems I was right. . . . But you'll never tell any of your secrets now."

He swung into the saddle once more, rode on till he picked up Buck's trail and followed it a couple of miles. But Buck had been wary of exactly this. Once he perceived he was not being closely followed, he had taken crude but effective means of covering his tracks. Kirk lost them on the edge of an expanse of flinty ground, and after half-an-hour's fruitless search turned back.

• • •

There was even more of a stir at the J Bar ranch, with the news of Eph Gowan's murder, than there had been at the time of Pecos Johnson's passing.

"It's pretty plain somebody's aimin' to knock us all off, one at a time," Buff Cleghorn commented to Kirk, his grey eyes flashing dangerously. "Mebby one of us better ride down an' have a plain talk with Buck Hutchinson!"

Kirk had thought it all over. He shook his head.

"There's not much doubt about Buck's part in all this. But it won't do to face him out till you're ready to kill him. He's a curly wolf, and he's ready for just such a play."

"So then what?" Buff countered bluntly.

But Kirk only frowned.

The disposal of Eph Gowan's remains was made as quietly as possible. Once more Joan preferred to keep the matter from Dickie's thoughts. It was at Kirk's suggestion that a couple of punchers packed the old man down the hills to the desert basin which once had been his home, and there buried him near the sand-buried remains of his one-time ranch house.

Meanwhile Dickie Jordan went his serene way without a thought save his own concerns. If the sober abstraction of his elders made any impression on him, it was only to note that they paid less attention to his comings and goings than usual.

He had done a great deal of thinking about his grandfather since the one visit he had made to the lower ranch. More than once he had turned his pony's head that way, only to be deterred by his father's command that he should not go down the hills again. He obeyed, but it was a strain.

His childish mind kept turning over the question: Why? Was there any reason why his grandfather must be left severely to himself? And what could it be? Grandfather Cole had been good to him. He was good company. Dickie mightily wanted to enjoy more of that same company, for he suspected that the two of them shared an understanding unknown to his mother and father.

These things continued to bear on his thoughts. He found no answer to them, and no lessening of his desire to look into his grandfather's stern but kindly face once more.

So it was that one afternoon he suddenly made up his mind to slip away once more. He set out cheerily. Nothing would happen to him, he told himself. He would come home earlier this time; no one need so much as know where he had been.

True, it was not as nice a day as that other had been. For some reason the sun did not show through very plain, and it was very hot. Had Dickie been older, he would have read the signs and known that a desert storm was brewing. But he was not, and he did not know.

He had not been gone an hour when his mother

went to the ranch house door to call him in before the storm's descent. That he was nowhere in sight did not cause Joan immediate concern; but before many minutes, having examined the near surroundings without result, she began to ask herself what had become of him.

"Surely he wouldn't wander away in this?" she asked herself, gazing at the by now angry-looking sky.

But it appeared that he had. Arriving twenty minutes later to look after things at the ranch, Kirk found her still fruitlessly searching the range with worried gaze.

"What's the trouble?" The question sounded elaborately casual in this strange silence of nature.

"It's Dick, Kirk—he isn't here!"

"How long have you been looking for him?"

"For half-an-hour at least." Her tone was frankly worried. "You don't suppose—?"

Kirk turned wordlessly away, going to see whether the boy's pony was in the corral. It was not. He came back, his face cast in lines of studied calm.

"Well, I expect there's only one answer—" He broke off, gazing at her blankly as a new thought struck him. But Joan was the one who put it into words:

"Kirk! He can't have gone down there?" She was thinking of the Ladder ranch—and of her foster-brother. Since the death of Pecos and of Eph Gowan, she had come to realize to the full how dangerous Buck really was. To let Dickie get within reach of him was little different from watching the boy walk into a wolf's den.

Kirk's tone was grim now: "I'm afraid that's exactly where he's gone!"

He turned and burst running toward the corrals. It was not many minutes before he had routed out every available hand. He flung instructions at Buff Cleghorn, cinching up his own saddle:

"He's headed for the Ladder outfit, but he may never get there! You boys can work down that way, but spread out—make sure you comb a wide stretch! And hurry—there may be some chance of spotting his tracks before the sand hits!"

He rode back to the house leading an extra mount. He well knew that Joan would refuse to remain home at such a time. But before they started out he barked at her: "Go get a veil to put over your head! And snatch a blanket or something to wrap the boy in! He may be all in when we find him!"

A moment later she was ready. Kirk grabbed the blanket, folded it and wadded it into the loop of his saddle strings. They set out. The punchers had already started.

The sky had a baleful look now. The clouds of dust hovering miles in the air over the desert wore a frown of fury. Kirk had never seen a more threatening outlook; he felt sure that not even the J Bar could escape this time.

"*Why* did he have to start down there now?" Joan groaned. "If it had been almost any other time—"

"He hadn't the remotest idea there was any danger," was Kirk's answer. "Perhaps he started soon enough to get down to the Ladder before the storm hits. . . ."

But he was only talking to allay his own bitter apprehensions. He was utterly unable to down the conviction that in his innocence the child was doomed.

Still the ominous sky grew darker and darker. It cast an unearthly hue over the range which seemed to presage terrible things. Even the faded green of the sagebrush was tinged a sanguine scarlet. The air was stifling, close. It felt scorching.

"Perhaps he will turn back," Joan tried to buoy them both up. "Even a child would know there was something wrong!"

"He may," Kirk nodded. He did not add his certainty that it would be too late.

But there was no giving up until every conceivable hope was exhausted. Presently a sinister mutter made itself heard, a kind of droning rumble. It drew closer. And now they perceived the brush bending before the scorching blast of wind; vagrant airs caressed them, and a faint whisper set up underfoot.

"Here it comes! Get that veil over your face!" Kirk grunted. He was adjusting his kerchief over his own nostrils.

The blast struck them suddenly. It stopped the broncs, for they were headed directly into it. But Kirk wouldn't allow that. He kicked his own into motion, and tugged at the bridle of Joan's. They forged on slowly.

It grew so dark as almost to cut off vision entirely. But for the downward slant which they followed, they might almost immediately have become lost.

Time dragged out. It became an endless struggle, with malign forces swirling around them muddily; sand cutting their skin and shortening their breath.

Suddenly a figure loomed before them darkly. Kirk gave vent to a cry. But it was one of the punchers.

"Seen anything of 'im yet?"

"No!" Kirk was hoarse. "Keep on looking!"

The puncher wasted no words. It would do no good; and breath was precious. He turned his pony away and with a dozen strides disappeared in the madly driving pall.

After what seemed an interminable stretch, Joan pulled close to Kirk's side.

"We're getting close to Dad's place!" she called

in his ear. She pointed to a ledge which both recognized as a landmark. The ranch could not be more than a hundred yards away.

They reached it at last. Sand swirled around the corners in savage fury, but near the wall it was slightly quieter. Here in the yard the sand was inches thick; but Kirk was scarcely in a condition to observe details. His every faculty was fixed on the answer to a vital question which would soon enough receive its answer: Was Dickie here, in the house, safe from the storm?

Though she had not been here during all the endless months since her father had turned her out, Joan gave no sign that she remembered she had been told never to return. Slipping out of the saddle she staggered, buffeted, toward the gallery.

"I'll go in and ask whether he is here!" she cried over her shoulder to Kirk.

He looked after her, sitting his saddle, too haggard of heart to dismount for the moment. Then he caught himself up. At least he could see to it that these wheezing, red-eyed broncs got a little relief. He slid to the ground, and gathering the bridles, led the animals toward a protected angle of the wall.

Joan had disappeared in the house. When Kirk turned away from the broncs he saw no sign of her return; but a shadowy movement at the corner of the house caught his attention. He whirled, and whirling, fell into a frozen crouch.

Facing him at less than a dozen paces' distance, his thick lips peeled back from his teeth, a hell of up-gushing rage and hatred in his implacable eyes, stood Buck Hutchinson.

24

No words passed between Kirk and Buck, there outside the Ladder ranch house. Both knew what this meeting meant. There was more than a touch of violence in the murky light through which their implacable eyes met; in the sand which swirled down like a shroud.

There was only this moment of recognition, bitter as death. Then Buck's horny hand slapped the leather of his holster. Kirk was scarcely behind him in action, but he was more deliberate.

It was the touch of madness in the moment which spurred Buck to a frenzy of haste as he threw up and blazed away. Lead droned by within an inch of Kirk's face; the flat crack of Buck's weapon was muted and dulled.

The explosion of Kirk's six-gun came immediately afterward. A red streak split the uniform brownness of the light. There was a distinct *smack* as the slug took Buck in the chest. He froze, choked, and with a look of incredulous amazement, pitched down.

It was not the heat of the day that made Kirk mop his brow as he sheathed his gun. For a moment, there, it had been nip and tuck; he had felt it in his bones that only the gods of chance could decide which one was to walk away unscathed from this meeting.

That it was himself struck him as a piece of good fortune not so much for himself as for his son. Dickie needed him now, if he ever did.

He walked forward and made sure Buck was dead. Even as he straightened, there was a slap of feet on the gallery. He glanced that way to see Joan burst to its edge, Cole Hutchinson at her shoulder.

"Kirk!" she broke out, tautly. "What happened? Are you all right?"

He nodded woodenly. But when he spoke, his flinty glance rested on Cole's craggy face.

"I never asked for this. Buck showed up around the corner and came at me before I could follow Joan in the house." There was a take-it-or-leave-it sound to the words.

Cole strode forward. "Uh-huh!" He looked down at Buck, an inscrutable old eagle. "Wal, I reckon it had to come sooner or later."

Beneath his secret amazement, Kirk realized that Cole was not displeased to see this blustering bully gone, though Buck had borne his name. Kirk jerked out words then, turning to what was to him an immeasurably more important matter:

"Dickie isn't here with you?"

Cole too, forgot the man lying before them. "Why, no! Joan asked me that. . . . What *did* become of him?"

Kirk's jaw hardened to the blow. "He headed for here before the storm hit—"

The old man visibly paled. "Good God! Yuh mean to say he's some'eres out in this?"

"I've got every one of my punchers combing the hills down this way," Kirk struck in swiftly. "It's just possible the boy has taken shelter under a ledge or something—"

Cole was deeply struck by the threat of tragedy here. Plain to be seen what his feelings were toward the boy!

He galvanized into action in an instant, turning toward the bunkhouse, where the punchers were holed-up to weather the storm. In a few minutes he had them tumbling out, saddling broncs and getting ready to join the hunt.

Cole came back to Kirk. "What's the likeliest corner to look fer him in. Did yuh spot his tracks comin' down?"

"No. But he was heading this way, pretty sure—"

The punchers came jogging forward, looming up through the obscuring dust like shadows until they were quite close.

"Where to, Cole?" one queried, his hoarse tones muffled in the bandana around his face.

"Work toward the hills," Cole rifled at him. "Spread out—but not too far to keep contact! We don't want to pass the boy!"

A moment later Kirk, Joan and he, swinging

into the saddle, set out themselves. For a ways they clung together.

The fury of the storm had increased to a blind savagery. The sand thrashed at them seemingly from all directions; with a few minutes' time it weighed down their clothes, their hats. The heat was intense, and as for air, there seemed not to be any. In no time Cole was twisted by an agony of coughing.

"Father, you oughtn't to be out in this!" Joan exclaimed. "We've never had anything like it before!"

It was the first word of solicitude which had passed between Cole and his daughter in years, yet he accepted it gruffly. Looking at her out of bloodshot eyes, he grunted:

"Somebody's got to find that boy! There ain't no such thing as can't! I aim to hold up my end!" He coughed again, bent nearly double over the saddle horn. But Joan added no more, seeing how much it meant to him. She was torn between her natural cares for him, and her fear for her son. Would Dickie ever be found?

Exactly similar thoughts wove through Kirk's brain. Beside them was one comforting reflection at least: "I don't have to ask myself whether Buck Hutchinson has got his hands on him," he mused grimly.

But the clutch of the storm might be as final. They were separated now, wandering through the ruthless, swirling pall, hoping against hope. All they could depend on was that one of them might fall over the boy in his path. For the visibility was so poor, and the buffeting of the sand so violent, that they could none of them hope for an awareness of more than a small circle immediately around them.

In an hour's time Kirk's nostrils and throat were swollen and acutely painful. His face was raw from the eternal blast. It was all he could do to use his eyes. He opened them momentarily every second or so, then after a sharp glance around, allowed the lids to drop together.

He knew the others were in no better case. This was more than Joan should be forced to stand; but he was well aware she would not have had it otherwise.

It might well prove to be Cole's finish if it did not come to an end soon. Yet it was the old man's choice. Kirk sensed in Cole's driving intensity that the other had found something in Dickie's existence without which he was not greatly interested in going on himself. It was a revelation. For the first time he saw his wife's father in a completely human light.

The hour bred insight of a brand wholly foreign to normal life. Never before had Kirk soberly considered how it would feel to face the future without a son, knowing Dickie was dead, as he would if the boy were not found soon. Yet he was considering it now. It left a leaden weight on his chest. But he knew this to be as nothing compared to the sorrow his wife would have to support.

Somehow they would have to pick up the broken threads and go on, he knew. . . .

But while these somber thoughts raked through him, not for an instant did he relinquish the idea of searching furiously until his last breath was ready to leave his body. There was always the chance that at the last minute, Dickie would be found.

It was so that he was found, and almost by accident. Cole was the one who found the boy.

He had known himself to be on his last legs, and ignored the knowledge with a find of fierce scorn. No care was too much for him to take. He examined every gully and brush clump with automatic thoroughness.

It was by turning back for a second look at a low rock that he saw what he at first took to be black grass, blown about in the storm's fury. Then he let out a whoop: "A hoss, by Godfrey!"

It was Dickie's pony, all but covered over by the sand as he lay on his side. The fight had been too much for the animal. Even as Cole slipped staggering from the saddle, the "rock" moved— and he saw that it was the boy, huddled beside his horse, the saddle blanket over his head. Dickie looked out from its under-edge.

"O-o-oh-h, Drandfather," he cried, joy in the words. "I'm glad you found Dickie! I was getting skeered!"

Cole swept the youngster into his arms almost fiercely, as if tearing him away from the storm. But his own strength was almost spent. The boy held against his chest, he leaned against his mount and drew his six-gun, to shoot three spaced shots into the air.

They were muted and speedily lost, but Kirk and Joan were both close enough to catch the thread of sound. They appeared in a few moments. It was all Joan could do to keep from snatching the boy out of her father's arms. But Cole saw how she felt and handed Dickie over.

It was a thankful reunion there in the midst of the battering storm. Cole was all but used up; Joan was in little better case, and even Dickie was nearly worn out, and more frightened than he desired to confess. His father took him in a strong arm and turned to his bronc.

"We'll have to get out of this without losing any time!" was his wind-whipped comment.

He put Dickie in his saddle, then helped his wife and her father to mount. Swinging up behind the boy, he turned his pony's head then and began to lead the way back toward the Ladder ranch.

It was a far from easy task to arrive there, but an hour later they did so. Kirk was thinking about the many punchers fronting the storm, about whom something would have to be done, when Buff Cleghorn put in an appearance.

"We've got the boy, Buff, safe and sound—"

"Bueno!" the other exclaimed. "That's what we want to hear. I'll take a *pasear* out and tell the rest of the boys to knock off." He turned back into the storm.

Spent and beaten, Kirk made his way into Hutchinson's ranch house behind Joan and Cole. Buck had been moved from where he lay in the yard, and no one made mention of him as they gathered in the big main room.

Even here the dust penetrated, a thin cloud; but the air was so much lighter than that outside, where the storm still howled, that they breathed it with relief.

No words of blame were directed at Dickie. All were so glad of his being saved that the cause of it all was passed over in silence, save for the boy's grandfather saying:

"Remember this day, my boy; and when you see another such, you'll know there's danger for horse and man in it—"

Dickie's steady regard was candid. "Yes, Drandfather. If I forget, Daddy will remind me," he added confidently.

Kirk's chuckle was brief: "I'll remind you with a paddle!"

No words of reconciliation had yet been spoken between Cole and the others. At the call of necessity they had worked together without question. But now an awkwardness settled over them all. The earnest thoughts of six years were not to be brushed aside so easily.

Cole was the first to speak up: "Kirk," he faced the other bluntly; "I want to say I don't blame yuh for what happened today."

Kirk stammered: "You mean—"

Cole nodded. Buck was in the minds of both.

"He was no good to me, ever; and no true son. I thought he'd pull out of it in time—but it was no go. But for him—"

"Don't say any more, Father!" Joan broke in, desiring to spare him as much as possible. "We all understand. It happened this way and can't be helped now—"

He scowled. For a moment, the old habit of domination threatened to break through. Then he smiled grimly under his mustache.

"I will speak!" he insisted stubbornly. "I've had this on my chest too long a time. Buck was no good; but it's my fault, even more than his, that all the blood has been spilt in this country! *I* jumped Eph Gowan, an' wiped his ranch out; *I* let Buck rare into every man who ever showed an inclination to settle this range! It was up to me to stop his dirty-work—and I didn't!"

He looked out the window, and then waved his hand that way. "Look at that! Hell itself closin' down on me! . . . It's well deserved," he added

251

gruffly, after a moment. "I reckon the Lord's vengeance is in this. I've made deep scars on the range, an' now the desert's comin' to cover 'em." His hand dropped. He looked suddenly older, broken. "I reckon it's time for me to go."

Joan looked startled. "Go? What do you mean?"

His look was lusterless. "There'll be no grazin' this land after today. Most of my herd'll be wiped out—there'll be mebby enough steers left to pay off the boys. . . ."

"But where will you go, Father?"

Cole lifted his leonine head. Instead of seeing the wall, he appeared to be looking into a bleak and cheerless future, where nothing but the retribution of emptiness awaited him.

It was Dickie who broke the portentous silence: "We'll be doin' home soon as the storm lets up, Drandfather," he piped. "Why not tome up with us?"

Surprise flickered in Cole's worn cheeks. His eye fell on the boy fondly, then lifted to Kirk.

Kirk nodded as though to an unspoken question. "You can do that, Cole," he seconded quietly.

That Joan had been following the exchange anxiously was plain from the love-light in the gaze she turned on her husband. Cole was looking at Kirk too, with eyes unaccountably dimmed.

"I'll—do that, Kirk," he said huskily. "It's mighty decent of yuh to want me!"

He thrust out his hand. The two men shook.

• • •

Happiness came to the J Bar ranch in overflowing measure in the days which followed. The sun returned, and with it the promise of better seasons. The storm had struck here only slightly, its damage negligible. Kirk knew it might be years before another such storm befell; perhaps never.

Cole fitted into his place with admirable tact. By no words or sign did he reveal that he felt his position. He was the same occasionally irascible and opinionated old fellow whom he had always been. He delighted Dickie, who now found a worthy successor to Uncle Pecos in his affections.

The two seemed to be always together; they had chuckling secrets, and important projects between them, in which others were not included. One day Kirk saw them ride down the hills side by side, the old man and the stripling. He followed, even to the extent of watching them take the trail leading to the old Ladder ranch basin.

They spent hours down there, that day and other days. Kirk had no idea what they were up to, but that they were getting along so well together was enough.

What they were doing, was planting grass and pine seedlings and other growths, there in the barren basin. It was as exciting as a game to watch their success in this dogged fight with the sterile desert.

It was a long drawn-out business, but not even the boy's interest waned; for Cole had told him the story of this desolate spot, and it captured Dickie's imagination. He felt that they were partners in making reparation for Cole's earlier mistakes.

Their endeavors extended over into the following year, nor was it until then that, one day as they reined in, side by side, on a ridge overlooking the lower basin, Dickie surveyed the land below with brightening face and at last said happily:

"Well, Grandfather, it's been brown down there a long time since the grass died. It's getting green again now, though."

There was a contemplative contentment in the eyes of the seasoned, white-haired man on whom so many years seemed now to rest more lightly.

"Yes, Dickie," was his answer, "she's gettin' green again."

Center Point Large Print
600 Brooks Road / PO Box 1
Thorndike, ME 04986-0001 USA

(207) 568-3717

US & Canada:
1 800 929-9108
www.centerpointlargeprint.com